NOTHING INTERESTING
EVER HAPPENS TO

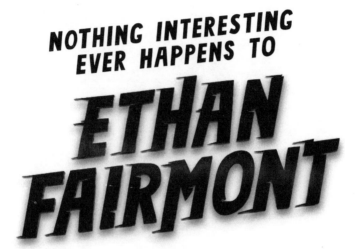

ETHAN
FAIRMONT

NOTHING INTERESTING
EVER HAPPENS TO

ETHAN FAIRMONT

NICK BROOKS

union
square
kids

NEW YORK

union
square
kids

NEW YORK

ISBN 978-1-4549-4557-4 (hardcover)
ISBN 978-1-4549-4558-1 (ebook)

Library of Congress Control Number: 2022010238

For information about custom editions, special sales, and premium purchases,
please contact specialsales@unionsquareandco.com.

Printed in the United States of America

Lot #:
2 4 6 8 10 9 7 5 3 1
07/22

unionsquareandco.com

Created in association with Cake Creative LLC

Cover illustration by Godwin Akpan

Dedicated to the inventors, young and old

HANDY-BOT 2.0 IS BUGGIN'

The problem with guinea pigs is that they aren't that helpful. I took a deep breath. "What do you think, Nugget? Should we try again?"

The guinea pig on my head squeaked, then continued chewing a piece of lettuce. "That's all you've got, huh? No words of encouragement? No inspiring speech?"

We stood in the middle of my bedroom. If you could call it that. Depending on who walked in, the room looked different. To Dad, it was his workroom. To Mom, it was the laundry room. To my brothers, it was an attic. But for me, once I pulled shut the curtains I'd installed along the ceiling, it was just me, my bed, and my projects.

Oh, and Nugget.

The above-mentioned guinea pig sat on my head in the custom Piggy Pack I'd built for him out of Dad's hard hat and an old cup holder. A little harness kept him secure as I circled my latest project and checked it for mistakes. You can never be too careful when building your own robot.

I pressed RECORD on my voice recorder.

"Trial number thirty-two for Handy-Bot 2.0. Today's objective is for Handy-Bot 2.0 not to explode. Yes, a moment of silence for Handy-Bot 1.0. By the way, we still haven't found the other arm, Nugget."

Nugget gave a sad squeak. Well, it was like all his all other squeaks, but I knew he'd slipped some sadness in there.

I took a deep breath. "Okay. Power on."

Oh yeah, I forgot to mention. Handy-Bot 2.0 is voice-activated. The last Handy-Bot, the one that exploded, understood my command to cut on—but not off. Every time, the bot would clean and clean until it overheated, then during one trial it finally exploded. I quickly realized that the Handy-Bot design needed a backdoor. Not a literal back door, but a way to shut the bot down manually when it was out of whack. That's one thing you have to remember with tech, always install a backdoor.

Handy-Bot 2.0 whirred to life. The robot was the size of a vacuum cleaner, which made sense because I took apart our vacuum cleaner to build it. It had two floppy arms made out of the vacuum hose, with a suction tube at the end of one and a rotating brush at the end of the other. I built its head out of an old computer monitor and a scuffed-up motion detector I'd found at the Sanctuary.

"Handy-Bot, online," the machine said. "Dirt detected. Now cleaning."

The robot zoomed around the room on its wheels, scrubbing and cleaning.

I grinned. "Trial thirty-two seems to be a success!"

Handy-Bot beeped and turned to look at me. "*Cleaning you next*," the machine said.

"Oh, no. Oh, no-no-no-no-no!"

I'd committed the ultimate unthinkable. The cardinal sin of science. The gravest of goofs.

I'd spoken too soon.

Nugget squeaked in dismay.

Handy-Bot raised both arms. The winking red light on its head lasered in on me. "Dirt detected. *Eliminating*." The robot rumbled across the floor toward me.

"Power off," I said.

But Handy-Bot kept coming. It avoided a pile of clothes near its wheels and then rolled over one of my plant-powered lamps.

"Handy-Bot, off!" I shouted. "Handy-Bot quit! Handy-Bot halt! Freeze!"

The robot didn't listen. I ran around and hid on the opposite side of the bed so I wouldn't be cleaned out of existence by my own creation.

Handy-Bot rounded the end of the bed. I jumped over the bed and fell face-first onto a pile of dirty towels, sending my Piggy Pack flying. Gross.

I peeked over the bed. Handy-Bot had stopped and was trying to vacuum something. I let out a sigh of relief. At least I had time to think now.

An indignant squeak came from on top of the bed. My eyes nearly fell off my face.

"Nugget!"

The guinea pig scampered around over rumpled sheets and lumpy pillows, dodging and ducking as Handy-Bot tried to vacuum it up.

Whump.

Handy-Bot held up its suction-tube arm. There, on the end, sat Nugget, the vacuum tube stuck on his butt.

I'd had enough. No one cleaned my guinea pig. Not even me.

"Handy-Bot," I yelled. I grabbed a ruler off my desk and a pillow off my bed. My sword and shield. "HANDY-BOT. Stop cleaning that pig's butt!"

I charged. "AHHH!"

I tackled Handy-Bot with a thud and used the ruler to flip the backdoor power switch I had installed on this model.

Nugget popped out with a plop.

"That was a close one, right, Nu—"

"Ethan Edgar Fairmont! You know I'm trying to sleep! Have you lost your mind?"

Mom stood midway up the stairs of the attic. She looked angry.

She wore her bathrobe and carried a mug of coffee in her hand, even though it was nearly two in the afternoon. Her deep brown forehead crinkled with annoyance. Mom worked nights at the Ferrous City hospital, so her routine was different from most mothers. Her discipline wasn't, though, and I wondered how to talk myself out of this one as she continued up the stairs.

"Well?"

"Uh, I can explain," I said, brushing myself off. "Actually . . . I probably can't explain."

Mom sighed. "You're supposed to be helping Mrs. McGee."

"I am," I said. "Sort of."

Mrs. McGee is our next-door neighbor. She's nice enough, I guess, but she had an accident a few months ago. She slipped on some wet leaves while taking groceries into the house. She bruised her knees and had to get a walker to move around on her own. She lives alone, so Mom started checking on her from time to time. Then Mom found out that nobody else ever came around to help her, so Mom started visiting every day. But when the hospital asked Mom to work longer hours, she asked me to start checking on Mrs. McGee. Not exactly how I pictured my summer of awesomeness starting out, sitting in a stuffy old house listening to scratchy records and doing crossword puzzles. Not to mention, her house sort of smelled like mothballs.

But it's not like I had a choice. So if I had to help, I decided to do it the only way I knew how, with an invention so magnificent, they'd *have* to hire me at NASA.

Arriving in my room, Mom eyed Handy-Bot and then gave me one of her *looks*. If I understood it correctly, this was her You-Had-Better-Know-What-You're-Doing look.

"You should be outside with your brothers instead of up here with this hamster."

"Nugget's a guinea pig, Mom. Besides, all Troy and Ant ever want to do is play basketball, and that's not me."

"Well, maybe you should go introduce yourself to the new neighbors across the street. There's a young man there about your age."

"Aw, Mom—"

"Don't you 'Aw, Mom' me. You were new to the neighborhood yourself once, Ethan. Remember how Kareem took to you? It's time to do the same. Speaking of Kareem, I haven't seen him around in a while. Have you checked on him?"

The traitor. I clenched my fists just thinking of the name. I ignored the question.

"Well, you see, Mom, I actually have plans today."

"Oh, really?" She sounded curious. "What?"

"I'm working on my greatest invention yet."

We both turned to the slumped-over Handy-Bot, and I had to admit, he wasn't looking too good.

"That thing?" Mom asked.

"Yes! And Mrs. McGee won't even have to reach down to turn him on and off. It's voice-activated! Just needs a little tweaking."

Mom looked at me skeptically.

"Okay. Well, find some time to include your new neighbor."

"Fine." I sighed.

Things were different in the summer. Our house was small enough; but now that summer was here, the twins were back from college. My older brother Chris and I were out of school, and Dad still hadn't found a new job; the house was crammed.

Two adults and four boys in a two-bedroom house, and I was the youngest. Being the youngest means you don't get a place to call your own. Dad needs work space? Move your books, Ethan. Mom needs to store her extra uniforms somewhere? Move your guinea-pig cage, Ethan. So now, every summer, I spend most of my time in the Sanctuary.

I grabbed my backpack and stuffed my sketchbook and yesterday's dinner inside. I ran over, kissed Mom on the cheek, and started down the stairs. You have to know when to stop talking and make your getaway.

"IS THAT MY VACUUM CLEANER?!" Mom yelled as I sped down the steps.

See?

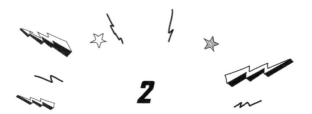

THE SANCTUARY
(*SHHH,* DON'T TELL ANYONE)

Our house sat at the bottom of a long, slanted block that faces east. I knew that because every morning the sun hit my eyes, trying to burn them or something. I darted through the yard. We were on the corner lot, so we had more yard than most of our neighbors. But no worries; I planned to add a mowing attachment to Handy-Bot to keep me from having to cut the lawn all summer.

I headed up the quiet block, which always felt like a workout. The sidewalks turned this way and that, sloping up and dropping suddenly down as if they couldn't make up their mind. A few neighbors sat on their porches reading their newspapers, while others watered their lawns. My neighborhood was kind of asleep, if a neighborhood could wake up and go to bed. Most of the people who lived around here were older, like

Mrs. McGee, and their children were all grown up with families of their own. I liked it this way—not too many forced interactions with neighborhood kids. Who wants to do all that talking? I was too busy.

At the top of the hill, next to the last house on my street, was a fenced-off field. Overgrown weeds and small trees crawled in and out of the fence. It looked like a giant green wall. But if someone was clever enough—say, a genius inventor with time on his hands—there were ways to sneak onto the field.

The sun had started to sink to the west by the time I snuck around several droopy bushes and behind a rotting tree. I heard something rustling in the bushes down the street, so I turned to make sure no one was following me. Several seconds passed. It looked like the coast was clear.

The fence the city put up surrounded the Sanctuary, except in one particular spot just big enough to crawl under. I hated crawling because I'd scraped my arm on the sharp edges of the chain-metal once. Wasn't pretty. So, with necessity comes invention. I pulled my Magna-gloves out of my backpack and connected them to a power pack, one of almost a dozen that I've put together.

I've got to say, the Magna-gloves were one of my coolest inventions. Biker gloves, super-strong magnets, and a little power, and you can climb any metal surface like a giant bug. A giant, awesome bug. I was over the fence and off to my stash in three seconds.

Now, the Sanctuary requires some explaining. Not because of where it is, but because of what it is. See, my secret hideout is an abandoned car factory, but not just any old, regular factory. I'm talking about THE Factory.

Ferrous City was built around The Factory. The town divided into two halves: East End and West End. A river separated them, with the factory sitting on the east side, where I lived. Dad told me once that they built it like that a long time ago so that the river could help power part of the building. But again, that was a long, long time ago, before video games and probably the Internet, too, I think.

Everybody worked there, and I mean just about *everybody.* If your parents weren't on the assembly line, they answered the telephones or sat at the front desk or cleaned it as janitors. Dad worked on the line when he was a teenager. His father and mother worked on the line, too.

So when The Factory shut down a few years ago, it felt like we all lost a home. It was no longer The Factory, said with emphasis and pride, but just the factory. Like it had all of a sudden shrunk down.

I cleared the field and jogged across the cracked parking lot. The front door of the factory and all the windows were completely boarded up. But there was a back door that only appeared to be shut. A closer look would reveal a movable piece of wood that opened the building to visitors. I approached the back of the enormous brick building, ducked under the boarded-up door, and slid aside a fallen table. Inside, the air felt dusty and heavy. I pulled out a scarf and tied it around my face until only my eyes were exposed. Always come prepared. Take note.

"Now, then, where are those old speakers?" I asked myself.

For a while, the inside of the factory had become Ferrous City's unofficial junkyard. People left their old gadgets and gizmos, whatsits and doodads, and whatchamacallits everywhere. I mean, it was a graveyard of parts, electronics, and, quite honestly, treasure just waiting for an inventor like me to breathe life into it. Things were quiet here. I could think. I could build. I was free, unlike in my cramped-up house. This was my . . . Sanctuary.

The factory was one long, open room, like a warehouse stretched out over a football field. Then again, I never actually played football, so I wouldn't know. At the very front of the factory was a little hallway with small rooms on either side. One had a sign that said SUPPLY ROOM, and the other said STOREROOM. If the factory were a plane, this was where the captain sat. In the back of the factory were stairs that led down to the basement. I didn't visit the basement much, not because I was afraid or anything. That's ridiculous.

The main floor was littered with piles of junk. Some piles were so high, you couldn't even see over them.

I moved through the dusty, cluttered factory floor to a storeroom in the rear corner. The roof had a fresh hole in it, letting in a stream of sunshine. I stopped and stared at it. "That's new," I said to myself. My Sanctuary was falling apart.

I felt a pinch in my stomach. I had a huge stash here; I couldn't lose this place.

I rummaged through old parts, glancing at the long work-table that hosted a collection of some of my other experiments-in-progress. And, to be honest, some of my failed experiments that didn't fit at home. Combination panini maker and waffle iron. Car muffler that makes bubbles. My favorite, even if it didn't work yet: a miniature greenhouse, complete with grow-lights. The grow-lights worked, but I couldn't get the humidity right. But none of this was what I was looking for with regard to Handy-Bot. I scanned the whole room. Far on the other side, I spotted the intercom speakers I'd tossed aside on an earlier trip.

"Bingo! That robot is going to win me a Nobel Prize in Physics."

I usually wasn't concerned with awards. The thrill of watching an invention work was validating enough. Although, I did win first place in the citywide science fair once. But when, well, when the traitor left, I tossed the trophy we were supposed to share into a garbage press.

Good riddance.

I filled my backpack with parts and odds and ends. Handy-Bot 2.0 would be my greatest invention yet.

Something scraped along the floor, and I froze.

What was that?

The noise came again. This time from my left. It was near the entrance. Had someone followed me, I wondered.

I narrowed my eyes and clenched my fists. Spies! They were going to try and steal my ideas! Inventors always have to guard their secrets. That's why they write in codes with ciphers to keep other people from taking their ideas.

"Who's there?" I yelled.

Nobody answered. I slipped on my Magna-gloves and powered them up. Screws and paper clips and other small pieces of metal flew toward my hands. Soon each glove was covered in a wiggling ball of metal.

"I'm warning you," I yelled again. "If you don't leave, I'll pulverize you!"

To be honest, I was scared. Dad had told me time and time again about going to the factory, but I always ignored him. "You can get hurt in there, Ethan," he would say. "There are sharp objects in that factory," he'd warn. But never did I think I'd get *kidnapped*.

"Don't make me tell you again," I shouted, banging the metal on my gloves against an old filing cabinet I was hiding behind. "All right, here I come!" I started to yell like I was going to charge. I banged my fists faster. I raised my hands over my head like how red pandas do to make themselves look bigger when they're ready to fight.

Something shuffled near the entrance to the storeroom. A small head peeked around the corner. A mop of black hair fell over a brown face that looked nearly as frightened as I was.

"*Whoa!* Don't pulverize me!" the voice said.

I stopped yelling and banging. "Come out where I can see you," I said with bravery I didn't feel.

He came around the corner and inside the storeroom. I relaxed. The voice belonged to a skinny brown boy who looked about my age. He wore shorts and a white T-shirt smeared with red-orange stains. He must've shimmied through that hole in the fence. I turned off the Magna-gloves and put them away.

"Who are you?" I asked.

"Juan," came the reply. "Juan Carlos Hernandez. My family just moved here last week."

Oh, shoot. He's the new kid my mom told me to introduce myself to. And here I just threatened to pulverize him in a place I wasn't supposed to be with metal fists I'm pretty sure I wasn't supposed to have.

"*Uh . . .*" How do you do introductions? I struggled to remember what Mom always told me to do when starting a new year of school, before reality crashed down and I spent lunchtime hiding out in the library. "Hi."

Smooth.

"My name is Ethan." I stepped out from behind the filing cabinet and dusted myself off as if I hadn't been terrified just seconds ago. "I think I live right across the street from you."

Juan Carlos nodded. He was shorter than I was—then again, most kids were.

"Yeah, my grandmother said I should introduce myself. I saw you walking up the block and was trying to catch up with you," he said.

"So you weren't spying on me?"

"Spying? No."

He seemed sincere.

"Well, you should have spoken up sooner. I could've hurt you."

"I'm sorry. What were those glove things? And what's in your backpack?"

I threw my hands up. "What's with all the questions? For someone who said he's not spying, you sure do act like a spy." I took my backpack off and gathered up a few more parts. This Juan Carlos kid was annoying.

"Well, okay, then. See ya', I guess," Juan said, sounding disappointed.

Juan Carlos shoved his hands into his pockets and headed back toward the door. For a moment, I thought about apologizing and starting over. Just for a moment. But he didn't look back, so I shrugged and turned to grab a few more things. In case it wasn't obvious, I have never been good at making friends. Maybe I was missing that kind of programming.

Something rattled across the room.

"Don't touch anything on your way out."

The noise continued as sections of the junk pile began to shift and slide.

"Juan!"

"What?" a voice said behind me, making me jump. Juan Carlos peeked in from outside again. The junk pile continued to rattle, and my heart started to thud in my chest. If Juan Carlos wasn't making the noise, then . . .

The junk fell in heaps as something emerged from beneath it. Slowly, a giant silver orb floated higher and higher until it loomed over the factory floor, shaking and rattling as it came to life. It zoomed toward us. I could see it wasn't actually hovering—it was growing! As the orb gained on us, it expanded, as if preparing to swallow us whole.

Someone started screaming.

Me. I'm someone.

"Run!"

I turned to escape and almost bulldozed Juan Carlos.

"Wait for me!" he shouted.

I ran the fastest I've ever run in my entire life, and it still wasn't quite fast enough. I looked back, and the orb was barreling toward us with no plans of stopping.

As Juan Carlos and I bolted, our mouths were wide open, probably because we were screaming. It didn't matter, though, because I couldn't hear anything over the clanging of the metal monster closing in on us.

So this *is it. This is my legacy. Boy genius crushed by giant unidentified object.*

We could see the sunlight glowing right outside the factory door, almost there. The metallic heap started to turn a bright golden light. Then it made a low humming noise, like it was preparing to blast us! Juan Carlos must've heard it, too, because he grabbed my hand. I wanted to snatch it away; but when I looked at him, I could see he was even more terrified than I was.

I clenched Juan Carlos's hand, dug deep to accelerate, and gave it my all as we lunged out the factory door, crashing through the loose wooden planks and landing outside with a thud. We curled up in a ball and closed our eyes tight, expecting to be squashed.

But we weren't.

I opened my eyes and the monster was gone. Well, it wasn't gone, but we could hear it clanging its way around the factory floor. Surely that thing could have blasted its way out of this old brick building, but it didn't.

Why?

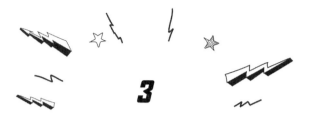

DO PEOPLE BELIEVE YOU? NOT ME.

Juan and I sprinted across that factory field as fast as our hearts would carry us. As I ran, I tried to process what I had just seen. My science brain said extraterrestrial, but my regular brain said secret tech. My kid brain said it doesn't matter, don't go back!

"Ethan, Ethan, wait up!"

I looked back and noticed Juan was a few yards behind me. "Wha . . . wha . . . wha . . ." Juan stammered as he tried to catch his breath. I stopped for a second, only to realize I couldn't breathe either. We both needed to catch our breath.

I helped him out. "What was that?"

"Yes!"

"I . . . I don't know."

"We have to find help!" he yelled.

"*Shhh!*"

I surprised him when it came out. I surprised myself. I wasn't quite sure why I shushed him, but it felt right.

"Whatever it is, it seems to want to stay in the factory," I said.

"So we're just going to wait until it decides to come out?"

"Maybe it won't. Maybe it's not even dangerous."

"Huh!? Of course it is!"

I held up my hands; too much was going on.

"Okay, okay, just let me think!" I said. There was only one way to determine if our special friend was friendly or not.

"I think we have to go back in."

Juan looked confused.

"You're not thinking straight, bro!" Juan said. "There's no way I'm going back in there."

"Fine. Even better. But you can't say a word about this to anyone. Not until I can figure out what that was. I've never seen a machine like that, and I've seen *every* machine. Which means this is a discovery. A discovery, Juan! Now that may not mean a whole lot to you, but to me it does."

Juan Carlos shook his head. "If you say so, man. I'm out."

Juan walked off and I looked back toward the factory. I didn't need to sound the alarm if one wasn't needed. Not only was the factory invaluable to me, but if this was what I thought it was, I would go down in history as the first human to make contact with an extraterrestrial. How awesome would that be!? As long as I didn't get smashed or abducted in the process.

If I was going to do this, I wasn't nearly as prepared as I needed to be. I decided to head home and strategize on how to handle this thing. I pulled out my Magna-gloves and climbed over the fence. Juan slipped under pretty easily. I guess being small had its advantages.

Juan and I walked our separate ways home, which was pretty awkward because we were headed in the same direction. I hate saying 'bye too early.

It's a well-known fact that nobody believes kids. Adults don't trust us. They read their newspapers or scroll through their phones or turn up the car radio, and we have to sit back and stew in our issues. So why bother telling them anything? For the rest of the day at home, my dad kept saying I was acting weird—but he never asked why. Parents always think because they were kids once, that they know what's going on with you. So when I was looking out the window all afternoon and getting lost in my thoughts, they would say absurd stuff like "if you're bored, I have some chores for you to do." It never occurred to them that I was wondering if a mysterious creature followed me home. No imagination. Needless to say, by the time I spent the late afternoon worrying, ate dinner, and got ready for bed, my mind was made up. I would keep it to myself, and maybe even forget about it.

But when I woke up the next morning, it was all that was on my mind. Even if I told my parents—what would I tell them, anyway? I still didn't know what to tell *myself.* Nothing happened. Something happened. What had happened?!

These thoughts and more crawled around my head as I huddled beneath the covers in my bed trying to figure out what weird, alternate world I was living in. Some of my best thinking happens in the burrow of the warm blankets I create every night. It's safe. Bad things can't reach me there. But if I wanted to be the greatest inventor ever, I'd have to get out of this bed and head back down to the Sanctuary.

Someone banged on the door at the bottom of the attic stairs.

Now if only my family couldn't reach me.

"Ethan! Breakfast. Last call."

I grumbled but emerged from my shell of covers like an angry turtle. Last call meant that whatever servings of food Mom or Dad saved for you would be released to the rest of the family if you didn't claim them in ten seconds. And the rest of the family in this case meant my older brothers.

Not good.

The house smelled like fresh biscuits and potatoes and onions. My mouth watered. All of a sudden, the Fairmont Last Call Rule took on more importance.

"Coming," I yelled as I thundered down the stairs. I burst out of the door at the bottom and into the living room. Troy, the older twin by one minute, sat on our faded leather couch scarfing a plate of food. He didn't even use a spoon or fork—he used a biscuit to shovel food from the plate into his mouth, making weird grunting sounds.

"Gross," I muttered.

He grinned, a piece of potato stuck to his chin. "Delicious."

"Where's Ant and Chris?"

"Hoops. You going? Or you got more dweeb stuff to take care of?"

"Go stock cereal or something," I shot back.

Troy was wearing his uniform shirt and cargo pants. Since coming home from college for the summer, he'd taken up a job stocking shelves at Jorge's Bodega. He also worked out every day behind the house with a scuffed pair of dumbbells. He'd started to put on some muscle, and now he thought he was big time. He stood and handed me the empty plate.

"Here, run this into the kitchen for me, Matchstick."

I swear, you accidentally set one toilet on fire and you're labeled for the rest of your life.

"Run it yourself," I said.

"I would, but I've got to skate out for work. Besides"—an evil grin crossed his face and my heart sank—"it's your plate."

"You didn't," I yelled, as he cackled and slipped out the front door.

"Last call," he shouted before the door closed, and I stomped into the kitchen.

"Dad—"

Dad raised a hand and shook his head.

"Don't come in here whining," he said, rolling a mound of dough flat. "I called you a half hour ago. There's a plate in the microwave if you're hungry. Grab a biscuit, but leave the big one for your mother."

I clamped my mouth shut because I sure wasn't about to start complaining. Instead, I grabbed the plate and biscuit and started eating.

"So what's old Ethan got planned for the summer?" Dad asked. He started cutting the dough with a biscuit cutter, lifting the pieces, and dropping them onto a greased baking sheet.

"*Mrgh*," I said with my mouth full of delicious, fluffy biscuit. I couldn't tell him that all my plans had changed because of the alien I thought I might have found. I finished chewing.

"Nothing. Just as boring as paint drying over here."

"What about your project for Mrs. McGee?" Dad asked. "Weren't you making her some special cane or something?"

"That was the original idea. But I decided it would be more useful to build her a robot."

"Oh. Well, that's something."

I wanted to tell him that the robot was old news. There were way bigger things at stake: I mean, a giant junk monster just tried to eat me! But I couldn't tell him that, so I shrugged and took another bite of biscuit. Seriously, those things were delicious.

"Fine, I'll leave you alone. But you can't back out of that project for Mrs. McGee. She's counting on the smartest kid she knows."

I knew I was smart. My family knew I was smart. And I knew my family knew I was smart. And I knew that my family knew that I knew that they knew . . . you get the picture. But hearing my dad say those words out loud was different. It made me feel all warm inside.

"You think so?"

"No, I don't think, I know."

I scraped my plate clean and got up to put it in the sink. I grabbed a couple of biscuits for the road and dragged my feet back out of the kitchen. I had a big day ahead of me. Possibly the biggest day of my life.

GADGET BEACH

My brain knew I had to go back to the factory, but my heart hadn't quite caught up to it. The image of that floating orb terrified me, and the thought of setting foot in that factory shook me even more. I had to think of an alternative if I was going to fix Handy-Bot. Sometimes, if you were lucky, you could find some junk from the factory washed up along the west bank of the river. There was one section in particular I liked to search—a bend in the river where more whatchamacallits piled up than any other spot.

I called it Gadget Beach.

A flat section of sandy dirt stretched along the river. Boulders and thick trees surrounded it on either side. Tons of junk poked out of the ground, and even more bobbed in the river, trapped in fallen branches and huge tree trunks. Most people hate the mess, but it's another one of my favorite places.

I propped Handy-Bot 2.0 on a flat rock and glared at it.

"I should just leave you here," I grumbled. The robot slumped forward but didn't respond. I'd brought my power packs, but there was no way I was going to waste them before I fixed the bot. I dropped my backpack and pulled out a humongous duct-taped book. It was actually three sketchbooks stuck together.

My super-secret, trademarked, for my eyes only, inventor's sketchbook.

I'm still working on the title.

I made sure I was alone and then flipped to the second-to-last section. Somewhere around page 1,008, I'd jotted down a quick component idea. Where was it?

Robot cat? No. Robot calculator? That didn't even make sense. Robot command module—got it!

Now that both Mom and Dad were on me about the robot, I had to at least try to figure out this voice-command system.

"Okay," I said, laying the sketchbook on the rock. "Maybe it's the command receiver. If the microphone is busted, my commands probably aren't clear."

I checked the command receiver and, sure enough, the microphone was disconnected. I needed something to stabilize Handy-Bot's plug-ins when it moved around.

I talked to myself as I combed the riverbank. Gadget Beach could be fantastic, or it could be awful. That was the beauty of it. Water and electronics don't mix, but sometimes you got lucky. After I grabbed two or three promising piles of scrap, I lugged everything over to the rock.

"All right, if I can strap this here, these two pieces will work as one, and then . . . voilà."

I checked my sketchbook often. Good inventors always work out possible problems on paper before building things, and this design was pretty spectacular, if I did say so myself.

Finally, after a lot of wrestling, hammering, and a few choice words I still felt guilty about saying aloud, a large chest plate sat on the rock. I stepped back, wiped the sweat off my forehead, and grinned. Pretty spectacular, indeed.

I'd built a robot T-shirt. Sort of. More like a turtleneck, I guess. I dropped the chest plate over Handy-Bot's head and attached it to its shoulders to keep it steady. Two microphones were bolted where his neck would be. Or his ears. I wasn't quite sure how robot anatomy worked.

A twig snapped in the woods behind me. I flipped around.

"Who's there?" I shouted. I slammed my sketchbook shut and stuffed it in my bag. "I'm warning you, don't make me—"

"It's me! It's me!" Juan Carlos stepped from behind a boulder.

I groaned. "Come on, dude! Why do you keep following me?"

Juan Carlos wore a faded camo T-shirt with the sleeves ripped off, and jean shorts. I shook my head. The boy was going to get eaten alive by the mosquitoes out here. Yeah, it was warm, but a little sweat was nothing compared to summertime bloodsuckers. "Sorry," he said. "Some kids were after me and I saw you head off this way, so I decided to join you." He kicked at a pebble and stuck his hands in his pockets.

No. He wasn't getting off the hook that easily.

"Were you followed?"

He shook his head no.

"Well, I'm trying to work and you keep bothering me."

He looked up. "Did you build that huge monster thing to scare me?"

"What do you mean?"

"It just seems everybody around here wants to pick on the new kid." Juan nodded to Handy-Bot. "Obviously you build stuff, so I'm just wondering if you were trying to scare me yesterday or if we really saw what I think we saw."

"What do you think we saw?"

"Maybe a secret government machine?"

It was an interesting angle. I started to feel bad about the way I'd treated Juan. I certainly was no bully and didn't want to make him feel like he didn't belong. People made me feel that way all the time.

"I don't know what we saw, but no, I didn't build it. Working my way to that. That's why I need to go back."

"Alone?"

I looked at Handy-Bot.

"Not alone, with Handy-Bot."

"Does it work?" he asked.

"Does it work?" I spluttered. "Does it work? Of course it works, ya goof. You think I'd spend all this time on something that doesn't work?"

Juan Carlos shrugged, and I glared at him. The truth was, I had no idea if Handy-Bot 2.0 would finally work. I certainly hoped so.

I grabbed the power pack from my bag and loaded it into Handy-Bot. I started to flip the switch, paused, took a deep breath, then turned it on. The robot hummed to life, spun in place, then idled quietly on the rock.

Juan Carlos glanced at me, and I shrugged. "Handy-Bot?" I called out.

"Handy-Bot online," the robot said in a monotone, robot-y voice.

Okay. So far, so good.

"Handy-Bot, clean." I said.

"Target unclear," came the response.

"*Uhhh.*" I glanced around.

"Handy-Bot, clean the rock you're standing on," Juan Carlos said.

"Cleaning," Handy-Bot responded. It began to brush and vacuum the large flat rock I'd assembled it on. Juan Carlos laughed, and I smiled as the robot scrubbed the rock.

"See," I said. "I told you it works."

Juan Carlos nodded and started to say something, then quit. "Why hasn't it stopped?"

"Huh?" I turned to look. Sure enough, Handy-Bot was still scrubbing the rock, the spinning brush moving so fast it was a blur. The robot's dirt-collection tanks were so full, they could've burst.

"Oh no! Handy-Bot, off!" I yelled.

The robot powered off. Little clouds of smoke floated above his head. I sighed and kicked at a pebble. At least it had cut off. Progress.

"Wow," Juan Carlos said.

"Look, I know there are still—"

"That was awesome!"

"Wait, what?"

He jogged over to Handy-Bot and blew away the smoke. "Did you see that? Look at this rock! I could eat off it."

I gagged.

"I'm serious, this is so cool! A cleaning robot. I wouldn't have to sweep anymore. My room! I wouldn't have to clean my room! Dude, this is great. It's fantastic. It's . . . it's—"

"It's a hunk of junk," another voice said from behind us. "And we should trash it."

Oh no.

I knew that voice.

I flinched as three kids walked into view, one of them larger than the others. RJ.

RJ and his gang, still wearing their basketball uniforms, stood a few feet from us. And while there were three of them, I was focused on one.

Not RJ. Who cared what a bully and a boring star athlete with cool shoes thought?

Not Diamond, or Di as everyone called her. Who cared what the fastest kid in all of Ferrous City—as well as RJ's sister—thought?

But the last dude. Him, I glared at. Him, I balled my fists for.

Kareem looked everywhere but back at me.

Oh, yeah. My former best friend, aka the guy who dropped off the face of the earth, aka the boy who then popped up months later hanging out with the dude who always bullied me.

Him, I had eyes for.

THE ~~BEST FRIEND~~ TRAITOR

Picture your best friend.

No.

Picture the person you trusted the most, the person you told everything to, the person you shared chips with, the person you lent a dollar to because you knew they'd forgotten their lunch, or the person who gave you a dollar because Dad was trying this tofu thing now, the person you rapped along to your favorite songs with, the person you skipped class with that one time (but only that one time, and that was because the hardware store was having a sale on electronic parts).

Picture that person.

Now picture that person gone, with no explanation, upped and moved across the river, going to a different school, and now hanging out with the guy who called you "Ethan the Cretin" and made fun of the shoes you wore.

Which person was real?

Kareem had an Afro that resisted all attempts to make it neat. Mom called his dark skin "smooth like chocolate and peanut butter." He was tall and lanky (like me) and he hated basketball (like me), which was why we got along. *Had* gotten along. Now, seeing him in a basketball uniform and hanging out with RJ, I wanted to shake answers out of him, but Kareem still didn't meet my eyes, no matter how hard I glared at him.

"Hey, Cretin, what'cha got there?" RJ slurped an oversized gas-station ICEE and raised his eyebrows.

Di stood behind him, her fingers blazing across her phone, ignoring everyone. "Is that a vacuum cleaner?"

Kareem was studying the ground, avoiding my eyes at all cost.

"Did you hear me?" RJ asked.

Kareem checked his watch, looked up and saw me glaring at him, and ducked his head back down quickly.

"Hey!" RJ walked over, still slurping, and got in my face. "I said, what'cha got there?"

"Nothing," I said. RJ was unfair in all the ways life could be unfair. Girls loved him for some reason, teachers thought he was the best, and his muscles had muscles. What sort of twelve-year-old has muscles?

Not to mention he'd stolen my best friend.

"Doesn't look like nothing," he said, glancing over to Juan Carlos who stood silently behind me. RJ shook the ICEE, frowned, then tossed it at Handy-Bot. "Looks like a weird little robot. Right, Di?"

Di snorted but didn't look up from her phone.

"Right, KC?"

"KC?" I said in disgust. Kareem hated nicknames. We'd laughed at the so-called popular kids who dubbed themselves this or that. We used to laugh at them, that is.

"What, you don't like the name?" RJ asked. "I think it fits."

"Only thing it fits is your spelling ability," I muttered.

Di let out a choking laugh even as she continued to text on her phone. RJ flushed and narrowed his eyes.

"What did you say?" he asked, moving even closer. We stood face-to-face. RJ put a finger in my chest and pushed. "You say something?"

"No."

"Nah, I heard something. I definitely heard something."

"It was funny, too," Di said with a snicker.

"Be quiet, *Diamond*," RJ shot back.

"Don't get mad at me 'cause he roasted you."

"He didn't roast me. Did you, Ethan?" He pushed me again with one finger. I tried to back up but the rock that Handy-Bot stood on was behind me.

"Did you?"

"Leave him alone!" Juan Carlos finally spoke up. I winced. This wasn't going to help anything. To my surprise, RJ backed up, though, and I straightened.

"*Heeey*, I remember you. You remember him, Di? KC? This is the little dude we saw hauling trash earlier. Right? Is that you, trash boy?"

So this was the group of kids messing with Juan Carlos earlier. A pang of sympathy tugged at me. Nobody deserved RJ's attention, even if he did lead them straight to me and Handy-Bot.

"You just pop up where all the garbage is, don't you?" RJ's eyes flicked to me when he said the word *garbage*. My face grew hot.

"What, Cretin? You got something to say?"

I looked back at Kareem, who had his mouth open like he was going to say something but stopped when he saw me.

Whatever.

Who cares about the traitor.

"Just leave us alone," Juan Carlos shouted.

"Just leave us alone," RJ mimicked. He used his same finger to push Juan Carlos in the chest. Once. Twice. The third time, I expected him to push harder, and I think everyone else did too.

I don't think anyone expected Juan Carlos to slap RJ's hand away.

"Don't touch me," Juan Carlos growled.

RJ's eyes bugged open. Di made a silent "oh" face and moved closer. Not to help, but to see what happened next.

"Tough guy," RJ said with a whistle. His hand shot out like lightning and grabbed a fistful of Juan Carlos's shirt. "Don't you ever, in your cheap little life, put your hands up like you're gonna do something. You hear me?"

Juan Carlos tried to wriggle free, but RJ balled up his fist and hammered the smaller boy in his stomach. Juan Carlos made the sound of air leaving a balloon and slumped down. RJ tossed him to the ground.

I took a step forward.

"What?" RJ turned like he had eyes in the back of his head. "You up next, Cretin?"

"RJ," came a voice from behind us.

It was Kareem.

"That's enough."

"What? You sticking up for your old pal? It's enough when I say it's enough. Nobody hits me. Nobody!" RJ turned and aimed a kick at Juan Carlos, getting him in the shoulder. Juan Carlos grunted and fell backward.

"Hey," I yelled. "Stop it, RJ!"

"Shut up, Cretin," RJ said, and began to kick at Juan again.

I had to do something. RJ would pummel me into the ground if I ran at him, but I couldn't just let him beat up Juan Carlos! I searched for anything that could help, and my eyes fell on Handy-Bot.

Cheese and crackers, I hoped this would work.

"Handy-Bot, on!" I yelled.

RJ turned in confusion, then froze when Handy-Bot turned on.

"Handy-Bot, online," came the robotic voice.

"Handy-Bot," I shouted, sprinting past RJ and hauling Juan Carlos up by the wrist. "Clear tanks."

"Emptying tanks," Handy-Bot replied. Dust and pebbles shot out of its tubes, pelting RJ, Di, and the traitor. They screamed and hollered as I grabbed my backpack and raced away, dragging Juan Carlos. I was sure they'd be furious the next time we saw them, but you know what? They'd have to catch us first.

We raced through the thick trees surrounding the river. I'd walked through these woods many times before, but I'd never run full-speed through them. It was like an obstacle course. *Run. Jump. Duck.* All the while trying to keep Juan Carlos by my side. I looked behind me and saw RJ and his crew gaining on us. "Let's go, Juan Carlos! They're catching up."

I could hear the sound of RJ and his gang thundering through the trees behind us, shouting and hollering.

"Where are they?"

"Look!"

"They went this way!"

I tried to listen while I ran, to see if the traitor's voice was mixed in with the rest, but I couldn't tell. Plus my heart felt like the heaviest part of my body with the thought of leaving Handy-Bot 2.0 behind. It'd saved us. And we'd left it on the rock. Who knows what they'd done to Handy-Bot by now.

I staggered against a log, and Juan Carlos helped me over it.

"Where do we go?" he asked.

I wiped sweat off my neck and looked around. The only place I knew for sure we could hide was the factory just around the bend. It's almost like Juan Carlos read my mind.

"But what about . . . ya know?"

He was right. For all we knew, there was still some sort of junk monster in there waiting to gobble us up. I looked behind me and saw RJ and his goons gaining on us. There were no other options.

"You want to wait around for them?" I asked, pointing to our apprehenders. "We don't have much of a choice."

"Well, how are we going to get in there? That fence opening is on the other side!"

I sucked down a huge lungful of air and stood upright. "You've never hopped a fence before?"

"I mean, sure, but that fence is like twenty feet high."

"Eight, more likely, and I've got a secret weapon."

"Bolt cutters?"

"What? No. Never mind, just . . . look." I reached in my bag and pulled out the Magna-gloves. Juan Carlos's eyes lit up, and a smidge of selfishness made me pull them back a little.

"I'll go over first, and then you follow."

"You're going to let me use them?" he asked, and my mouth struggled to get the words out.

"Yeeeaaa—maybe. I mean, yeeeaaa—we'll see."

"Ethan!"

"They're custom-made for my hands," I complained.

He crossed his arms.

"Fine, whatever. Just wipe your hands on your shirt or something." I slipped on the magnetic gloves, powered them on, then hobbled to the fence and started climbing. Finally I tumbled over the side and began to work my way down. Once I reached the bottom, I looked at Juan Carlos.

"You know I wouldn't normally do this—"

"Ethan!"

"FINE!" I hurled the gloves back over the fence and winced as Juan Carlos fumbled with them. I turned and bit my tongue. I couldn't watch, so instead I started getting the door open. I had only ever entered through the back of the factory, which was much less secure. The lock on the front entrance was more sophisticated, but nothing I couldn't handle.

I put down my book bag and rummaged through it, tossing aside the tools I didn't need.

"Aha!"

I found what I was looking for: a paper clip. I broke it in half and unfolded one of the tips. I jammed both pieces in the padlock on the chain wrapped around the door and fished around. *CLICK.* I had it open in about thirty seconds.

Juan Carlos dropped to the ground, beaming from ear to ear. I looked at him.

"Gloves."

He handed them over, still grinning. I shook my head and put the Magna-gloves away.

"I can still sue you," I muttered, then held the door open and we both disappeared into the dark.

"Do you think it's still here?" Juan Carlos whispered. "That thing?"

"I guess we'll have to see." I adjusted the scarf over my nose and mouth to filter out the dust and smell. I handed Juan Carlos an extra scarf from my bag.

If I was being honest with myself, that thing had to still be here, right? Just yesterday, it seemed like it didn't want to leave. The image of the bright, shining orb flashed through my mind.

"You sound hopeful," he said.

"Maybe I am!" I said quickly. "Being curious isn't a crime!"

"So what is this place?" Juan Carlos asked, changing the subject. I led him down a flight of stairs and into a dripping, sour-smelling tunnel.

"Do you have anything in that bag that will, um, light the way?"

"Oh. Right." I fished out a flashlight. I had been trying to think of a way to improve it, but . . . sometimes a flashlight is just a flashlight.

"This is the basement of the factory," I said. "If my theory is correct, this corridor will lead us to the stairs headed up. Decades ago, they used the river to load up steel on barges and float them down to collection points. I think they dumped their waste here too."

"Oh," he said. Then, "It's really creepy."

"I try not to come this way often. It stinks."

We moved through the factory's bottom floor, where old equipment sectioned off by fading yellow chains lay forgotten. We walked up the steps to the main floor of the factory, where they used to assemble the cars. Everything seemed to be on the up-and-up. We sat down by the door, instinctively refusing to walk deeper into the factory where we'd seen the orb.

"Now what?" Juan Carlos asked.

"Now we wait," I said. "RJ and the rest of them can't stick around forever. Give it an hour or so and we can slip out through the back."

I rubbed my legs while we sat there. Running sucks, but I was used to it.

"Do you smell that?"

I looked up from massaging my knees. "Hmm?"

"Do you smell that?" Juan Carlos asked again. "Like something's burning."

Something tickled at the back of my memory. "I'm sure it's nothing. This place is full of smells."

Juan Carlos nodded, skeptical. Something rattled in the distance, and we both jumped.

"What was that?" he asked.

"I don't know," I whispered.

"You think—"

"No thinking!"

The rattle sounded again. My breathing was faster than Nugget's at feeding time. Except, instead of anticipation, I felt dread.

"Maybe they're gone," Juan Carlos said half-heartedly. He looked at me and, after a second, looked away. "Those kids. They could be gone, right? We showed them. We stood up to them."

Seriously?

I jumped up.

"Stood up to them? Get that mess outta here. That's something adults say. 'Oh, you should stand up to your bullies and they'll back down!' Baloney. I don't know what bully manual they're reading, but that's not how it works. You stand up to them, you get punched. *That's* how it works. There aren't any fairy tale bullies that magically disappear or become your best friend after you show them you aren't afraid. No, they *take* your best friend and make him a bully too, and then nobody believes you and you're stuck with an empty summer and an empty life!"

I was shouting now. Juan Carlos's eyes were wide, as I stopped suddenly and balled my fists up. Now I *did* want to go find RJ and at least try to punch him. Or the traitor.

"Ethan," Juan Carlos whispered. "Hey, Ethan."

"What!" I snapped.

He pointed. I stood there confused. Then he pointed again behind me and I turned. My jaw hit the floor. All the anger drained out of me as we stared in amazement.

There it was, the orb from yesterday, all the way at the front of the factory. Only it had tripled in size!

My anger shrank into a ball of determination. I was always looking for the next big idea, the next great invention, that life-changing discovery. No matter how afraid I was, I knew this was my moment.

"Come on," I whispered.

Juan Carlos gulped and nodded. Together, we crept toward the front of the factory floor.

CHEESE AND CRACKERS, OH MY!

The giant metal orb idled in place as we approached. It didn't hover or hum or glow like it had before.

"This can't be real," I whispered. I glanced over and raised an eyebrow as Juan Carlos pinched himself.

I took a step forward, but Juan Carlos waved his hand.

"Wait," he said.

"What is it?"

"Look. Something happened when you moved." He took a step of his own to prove it. "See?"

A section of the orb glowed as Juan stepped near it, then dimmed again when he took his foot away. He repeated it several times.

I tried, and the same thing happened. "Cheese and crackers," I said.

Juan Carlos frowned. "You're hungry?"

"No," I said, still looking around. "Well, yeah, actually; but that's just something my dad always says when he's amazed."

"Oh. Well. Cheese and crackers, I guess."

I took a step forward. The object glowed faintly. I gulped but kept going. With every step closer, the orb glowed just a little brighter. I motioned Juan Carlos to follow me.

"Nuh-uh. Where do you think you're going?" he asked in an angry whisper.

"To find out what that is."

I tried to sound tough. Brave. A scientist collecting data. I took one step. Then another step. And another. All the while the room growing brighter.

"I don't know if this is such a good idea," Juan Carlos whispered. "It's much bigger than yesterday."

"Probably just a defense mechanism to scare away predators. Look, I'm weirded out too, but have you ever seen anything like this? It's like—" I wanted to say the word *alien*, but it felt too soon. I needed more data. "Look. We can either go back outside and pray RJ doesn't pummel us, or hang out in here for a bit. Me, I don't wanna get punched. Do you wanna get punched? Again?"

Juan Carlos rubbed his stomach. "No."

"So, if we're gonna stay in here, let's investigate. Aren't you even a little bit curious?"

He shook his head. "Curiosity killed the cat."

I rolled my eyes. "That's why I have a guinea pig."

I swallowed a lump of something that totally wasn't fear. "Not getting punched today, Ethan. Cool. So let's get eaten," I said.

"What?" Juan Carlos whispered from right behind me. I ignored him and kept moving.

We made our way across the factory until we were right up on the giant metal ball. I slowly extended my hand, wanting to touch the object and feel it for myself.

Suddenly, something shifted in the corner of my eye.

"Cheese and crackers!" I yelled and jumped back.

"What, what, what?" Juan Carlos asked.

"Did you see that?"

"No! See what? Where is it? What?"

I pointed to a section of the factory floor behind us, but nothing was there.

"Nothing, maybe I'm losing it."

No self-respecting inventor shied away from understanding new things. My father's words replayed in my head—"the smartest kid they know."

I can figure this out, right?

I turned back to the metal ball, ready to touch its surface, when the last voice I ever expected to hear called out in the factory.

"Ethan?"

Juan Carlos tensed, and I clenched my hands.

Kareem.

He gawked at the metal orb.

"What are you doing here?" I asked.

He tried to focus on me, but his eyes kept getting pulled away to stare at the faintly glowing orb. "Ethan, what is that?"

"What. Are. You. Doing. Here?"

He turned to me and shook himself out of his daze. "I brought you this. Thought you might want it back."

Kareem reached outside the door and pulled in Handy-Bot 2.0. The robot was dusty, dented, and scratched. One of his tube arms had a rip that made it dangle uselessly, but otherwise it looked fine.

"Sorry about the scratches. Getting that thing over the fence wasn't easy."

I let go of a breath it felt like I'd been holding forever. Muscles I didn't know were tense released. I took a step forward, wanting to pull my robot apart and go over every piece, every component, and make sure it all worked and everything was okay.

Kareem wore the same half-smile I remembered from when we used to talk about comics or draw up our own role-playing games. He gazed around the factory, his eyes falling on my workbench.

"Still working on the greenhouse with the grow-lights?" he asked. "Did you ever get the humidity right?"

I stopped. No. He had no right to wear that smile.

"Yeah, well, you brought it. 'Bye."

The smile faded. "Look, I know you're probably upset—"

"Upset! Who's upset!? I'm not upset. I'm just busy. So leave and let us get back to what we were doing."

Kareem stared in confusion. "We?"

"Hi," Juan Carlos said, peeking out from behind me.

Kareem looked past me at Juan Carlos. Realization spread across Kareem's face. "Oh."

"Yeah, oh. The boy you watched get beat up by your new buddy. Where is RJ, by the way? Torturing some other middle schooler? Burning ants?"

"He's not that bad. I mean, he has his moments; but once you get to know him, he's different. I told him you probably went home. I didn't tell them about the Sanctuary."

I shook my head. "Oh, so you're the big hero now? You want a pat on the back? Well, forget it."

"Ethan—"

"STOP SAYING MY NAME! You don't get to talk to me like we're friends! We're not friends!"

Juan Carlos stepped next to me and put a hand on my shoulder. I realized I was yelling and forced my mouth shut. My fists were so tight, my nails were digging into my palms. Hundreds of questions raced through my mind. I wanted to ask them, but I also didn't want to hear the answers.

"We *were* best friends," I said, suddenly tired and wanting nothing more than to go home, feed Nugget, and read a comic book. "Not anymore."

"Ethan," Juan Carlos whispered.

"Best friends don't leave all of a sudden without telling each other. Best friends don't stop talking to each other. Best friends don't hang out with huge jerks. Best friends—"

Kareem pulled something out of his wallet and held it out. The words dried up in my throat.

A picture, wrinkled and creased from being folded. I couldn't see it from where I stood, but I didn't need to. I already knew what it showed. I had the same picture in a frame on the wall of my room. Well, I used to. I tossed it aside one night. The same night the first-place trophy went into the garbage press.

That picture was burned into my memory. Despite everything I tried, I could never dig it out.

It was a picture of the two of us, me and Kareem, at Ferrous City's regional science fair, beaming as we held the first-place trophy. Kareem had his arm over my shoulders, and I held up bunny ears behind his head. Our invention, The Food-o-Tron 1000, sat on the table next to us.

It was one of the happiest moments of my life.

A week later, Kareem moved across town and never spoke to me again. Until now.

"Is that supposed to make everything cool again?" I snarled. The room twinkled, and it took me a second to realize it wasn't the glowing orb, but my eyes were being jerks and making tears.

"No, but—"

"Just go, man. Get out of here!"

As I said the words, I kicked the orb—and I instantly regretted it. A booming sound echoed through the factory, and the metal ball started blinking in brilliant patterns.

"What's going on?" Juan Carlos yelled.

"I don't know! I don't know!" I panicked and dropped to the ground, trying to scramble away.

I looked up and saw something speed past again, but I couldn't make out the figure in the darkness.

A low rumble grew from the orb, like it was trying to power up.

"Ethan," Juan said.

I couldn't listen. I was stunned by the glowing machine in front of us.

Suddenly, the blinking stopped and the rumble faded out until all we heard was silence.

"Ethan!" Juan Carlos said louder, this time yanking on my arm.

"What?" I snapped. Juan Carlos ignored my tone and pointed. Kareem turned and froze.

Just behind him, where he'd dropped Handy-Bot 2.0, a creature circled my robot.

It was small—just a little bigger than Nugget—with metallic gray hair covering its entire body. It had six big eyes, three on each side of its head. It seemed to be young and curious. It circled Handy-Bot. I couldn't see any feet. The thing glided across the floor. Its tongue shot out from its face and prodded different parts of Handy-Bot 2.0—almost as if it was trying to figure out what Handy-Bot was, while we were trying to figure out what *it* was.

The creature turned to us and slowly slid forward, leaving the faintest trail on the floor, like a slug. As it moved in, it spoke really fast in a squeaky voice.

"Wh—what?" I asked.

It spun in a circle and bobbed up and down; then it tried again.

"Chee, cragger?"

I nearly passed out.

7

CLOSE ECOUNTERS

Everyone knows what an alien looks like. Skinny gray dudes with huge black eyes and an oversized head.

Right? Everybody knows that.

They don't arrive on Earth in glowing ships. And, above all else, they absolutely do not scuttle up to you and say, "Cheese and crackers." Or at least attempt to.

So, that left me in a bit of a pickle.

I sat on the dirty floor of the factory and stared in amazement as something clearly not from this planet squeaked in front of me. It twirled every so often, spinning in place as it bobbed up and down. I suddenly had the urge to draw it in my sketchbook. This was history! First contact!

It bobbed closer.

I should have been afraid. But I couldn't be.

"Chee-ah-crackers?" it said, followed by some more sounds I didn't understand.

I licked my lips. "My name is Ethan Fairmont. Welcome to Earth. I—"

Before I could finish, a door in the orb lifted and our little metal friend shot inside.

"What in the world is that?" Kareem asked.

"That's just it. I don't think it *is* from this world," I answered.

"An alien?" Juan Carlos whispered.

I couldn't believe it. But one thing about scientists, and inventors specifically, we never disregard an idea just because it's new to us. You could miss out on a lot of cool inventions that way.

"I think so," I said.

Kareem looked around, nervous and scared. "What do you think it's doing?"

"I . . . I don't know." As soon as I spoke, the door of the ship opened again and the little alien peeked out.

"Chee-an-crackers?" it said. Again, it spoke in that strange high-pitched voice, like when my brothers and I used to breathe in helium from balloons and talk in squeaks.

"What did it say?" asked Juan Carlos.

Kareem glanced at me, puzzled. "Did it just say—"

I nodded. "Yup. For some reason that's the only thing it can say, in English anyway."

When the alien saw that the three newcomers weren't going to charge its ship, it came out a little farther.

"Chee-an-crackers?" it squeaked hopefully.

I shook my head and slowly stood.

"Ethan," I said, pointing at my chest.

The alien spun in a slow circle. "Chee-an-crackers?"

"No, Ethan."

"Cheese—"

"Ethan."

"—crackers?"

I threw my hands up, which caused the alien to spin several times.

"Careful, Ethan," Kareem whispered. "No sudden movements. Let's get out of here."

"No way." I glared at Kareem, but the spectacle of an alien drove the anger at my former best friend out of my mind. Juan Carlos had a curious expression on his face, like he recognized something strange.

"Hey, I have an idea," he said. "Ethan, let me borrow some paper from your sketchbook."

"What?" I said, confused.

"Paper. And a pencil, if you have one."

I had no idea what he was planning, but I nodded and handed it over. Juan bent over a hunk of junk and started to draw pictures.

"What're those?" Kareem asked.

"When my parents first moved here, they took classes on the weekend with an English tutor. They wanted to learn the language as quickly as possible. The tutor would always bring pictures of basic, everyday things to help us identify what each word meant."

After a few minutes, Juan Carlos stood up straight and held up several drawings.

"You think those are gonna work?" I asked him as he walked over.

He bit his lip. "I think so. I went to a few classes with my parents in the beginning. You know, to help translate until they could understand for themselves. The instructors always used a lot of pictures about familiar things, and they'd repeat simple words and phrases and sentences."

I nodded. "You want to try it with the alien?"

"Yeah," Juan Carlos said.

He hesitated, then took a deep breath and moved in front of the alien. It bobbed up and down and waited. Juan Carlos held up the first picture of a rocket ship. It was a pretty good drawing.

He stepped closer, cleared his throat, and waved at the alien.

"Hi. Um, see this? Ship. Ship." He pointed at the picture and said the word slowly and clearly. Then he took another step forward and pointed toward what was obviously the ship. "Ship. I get in my ship. My ship flies through the sky." He moved the paper around like a kid with a toy.

The alien bobbed slowly.

Juan Carlos stepped forward again and held the picture closer. "Ship."

Nothing. I shook my head, and Juan Carlos frowned.

"Got one." Juan Carlos held up a picture of a house. Three stick figures stood inside, smiling, and he brought the picture toward the alien.

"Home," he said, pointing at the picture. "Where is your home? This is my home. I sleep in my home. Home."

Kareem and I glanced at each other, then at the alien, who bobbed up and down slowly. Then it twirled in a circle.

"Chee-an-crackers?"

Juan Carlos lowered the picture in disappointment.

"Hey, it was a good try," Kareem offered.

We all stood and watched the alien as it watched us. The novelty was beginning to wear off. I mean, aliens are cool, no doubt about that. And the spaceship? Incredible. But all those TV shows and movies about aliens and first contact never mentioned how to teach them our language. They always walked off the ship speaking fluent English. Or else there was some cute, two-minute video montage of the alien learning human culture.

Then a thought hit me.

"Show him home again. We may not be able to understand it, but maybe it understands us."

Juan showed the small alien the picture of home. The alien bobbed and twirled again.

"Maybe it wants to get home?" Juan said.

"That would make sense. But maybe it can't. Maybe we need to figure out why. It obviously needs our help, or at least is open to it, otherwise it wouldn't be so friendly."

We needed a video montage.

We also needed a name.

"What should we call it?" Kareem asked.

I glared at him. Ex–best friends weren't allowed to think the same thing at the same time.

"How about Cheese?" I said.

The alien bobbed quickly and twirled. "Chzwrzkrnpop?"

We all stared at it. "*Uhhh*," I said, confused.

"Cheese and crackers?" it said hopefully.

Kareem grinned. "I guess Cheese fits," he said. "Now what?"

"Maybe it's hungry." I reached into my pocket to pull out some of my biscuit from earlier.

Cheese bobbed up and down even faster.

"Chee-an-crackers!"

It twirled once more, then a hole appeared in what I believe was its face and, quick as a snake, what looked like a slimy arm zipped out and snatched the food right from my hand. It stuffed it in its mouth, and spun in a circle in what I guessed was excitement.

"Cheese and crackers!" I said.

The alien came even closer. Too close. I backed up and it followed, bobbing up and down faster now. Its mouth appeared again, wide and dark like a tunnel.

"Guys?"

Cheese followed me. A silver arm shot out again, and this time it stayed out, brushing the side of my jacket and feeling in the pockets. The arm didn't seem to be metal like the rest of its body, and thankfully I saw that the arm didn't come out of the mouth, but just below it. Actually, that made sense. If my chin could bring food to my mouth, that would free up my hands for more important things, like building stuff, or making more food.

Cheese felt around in my pocket and pulled something out.

"Hey," I yelled. Cheese bobbed and twirled and stuffed the rest of Dad's biscuit into its mouth.

"Chee-an-crackers!"

"*Ew*," I said as crumbs sprayed out. "Don't talk with your mouth full!"

After Cheese ate my biscuit, I noticed a dark spot on his head had cleared up. It was like he had been instantly healed.

"Guys," I said slowly. "I think I know what the problem is. Cheese is hungry. And I think it needs to eat more soon."

Cheese bobbed closer, and I turned out my pockets.

"Sorry, buddy, I'm all out of snacks. For real this time."

I reached in my bag and pulled out my favorite glass thermos.

"Here, have some water to wash it down."

Cheese bobbed up and down frantically like something had startled him. His arm shot out, ripping the thermos from my hands and launching it at his ship. The glass shattered on impact and water splashed everywhere as we all jumped back.

Cheese bobbed slower and the silver arm disappeared.

I looked over at Kareem and Juan Carlos. They both shook their heads.

"Okay, I guess you don't like water. Or glass. Or both. Y'all have any more food?"

"Sorry, my candy pouch is empty. RJ cleaned me out," Kareem said.

I raised my eyebrows in surprise. "You still have that thing?" That candy pouch used to go with Kareem everywhere, and at any given time of the day you might catch him slipping a hand inside to fish out a treat.

"Of course. Maybe we can go pick something up?" Kareem said.

"Jorge's is still open," I said. "We can get some food there. Troy is working today, so that means Jorge is working the griddle."

Jorge's Bodega not only carried food and other groceries, but Jorge had installed a flat-top griddle in the spring. On days in the summer when he had help, he'd cook a bunch of steak and chicken and shred them for tacos and burritos, then deliver them to neighborhood kids and the elderly folks who couldn't move around that much.

Juan Carlos brightened. "That's brilliant!" he said, dropping to his knees to retie a sneaker. "Cheese, you're gonna love this food."

The alien bobbed quickly. "Cheese and crackers?" It moved over to Juan Carlos and twirled near him. "Cheese and crackers?"

"Wait, no, I don't have food now—"

"Cheese and crackers?" Cheese hovered closer, and Kareem and I exchanged worried glances.

"No, I don't have food, we're going to *get* you food, not—"

"Cheese and crackers!"

The silver arm shot forward and grabbed Juan Carlos's foot and started to pull him toward its mouth.

"*Ahhh!*" Juan screamed as he slid toward the alien. Kareem and I rushed to grab his arms, but the thing was just too strong. It started pulling all of us!

"Don't let it eat me, don't let it eat me!"

"Stop screaming! I can't think!"

I looked around and noticed that the tentacle only had Juan's shoe. I rushed to his side, untied his shoe, and *swoosh*, Juan's shoe went flying off and into the alien's mouth. Cheese chewed on the toe for a bit and then spat the half-eaten shoe out of its mouth. Its stomach rumbled.

"*Auuugh!*" Juan Carlos shouted, scrambled backward, then took off running out of the room. Kareem and I ran after him so we wouldn't be next on the menu.

"Go, go!" I shouted, scooping up Juan's shoe as we all ran out onto the factory floor and out the door.

SNACKS MIGHT'VE BEEN A BAD IDEA

I ran a kids' marathon once. It was one of those fundraising races in the school gym where you did laps around cones and got a T-shirt if you participated. I only did it because RJ told me he was going to shove dirt in my mouth after school, so I borrowed some spare shorts, pretended to be excited about raising money for new cafeteria trays, and ran for as long as I could. If you stopped, they pulled you to the side, counted your laps, and sent you on your way.

Well, I didn't stop.

I ran thirty-two laps in an hour and fifteen minutes.

Somebody told me RJ got bored and went home, and I got a T-shirt and the knowledge that if I wanted to, I could run forever.

"Ethan, dude, stop. I need to . . . breathe," Kareem panted.

Kareem hadn't done the marathon, but he'd still come to the race. He cheered me on from the sidelines, slurping off-brand cream soda and shoveling hot cheese puffs into his mouth. He never did like running—which is partly why he hated basketball. And now he was on the team with RJ.

I held my side and waited as Kareem struggled to keep up, wondering again what had happened to the two of us. We'd been close. Road dogs. Brothers, even.

Juan Carlos came hobbling up.

"Look," I said, pulling out Juan's sticky shoe from my bag. "I saved your shoe, sort of."

Juan twisted his face as he cleaned the shoe with his shirt.

"We need to find Cheese some food, and fast."

"No, Ethan," Kareem said. "We don't. Dude, that is an alien back there. An alien! We have to tell somebody."

"Same thing I said," Juan chimed in.

"Tell them what?" I asked. "You think anyone is going to believe an alien from outer space flew to Earth in a giant glowing orb and is eating our shoes?"

Juan Carlos sighed loudly and stared at the puddle he'd just stepped in. His sock was soaked. He ignored both of us as he tried to shake the water off. Finally he took his sock off and dangled it from the back pocket of his shorts.

I shook my head and started walking up the block again. After a few seconds, the other two followed. The cramp in my side throbbed, but I gritted my teeth and kept moving. We cut through a few backyards and alleys, and I couldn't help but notice how weird everything looked, like the color had been sucked out, and we all lived in one of those black-and-white photographs Mom kept taped to the mirror above her dresser.

Kareem caught up with me and rubbed his 'fro. He used to do that all the time when he was working through a problem. Some things never changed. But only some things.

"I don't know, man," he continued. "I still think we should tell somebody."

"Who? The cops?" I asked. "You want to tell them? They'll just capture Cheese and do experiments! They'll hurt it."

"No, not them. But—"

"Our parents? They'll just ground us for being in the factory in the first place."

A weird look crossed his face. "NO! I didn't say that!"

I raised my hands in a calming motion.

"Okay, well . . . who, then? Who are we going to tell? And why? Cheese didn't do anything to anybody."

At that moment, Juan Carlos yelped as his bare foot stepped in something hidden in a clump of weeds. He bent down to stare at his foot, sniffed; and then his eyes grew wide and he started to shout and hop around like he was on fire.

Kareem watched, then turned back to me and stuffed his hands in his pockets. "Why do you care about it so much? You always hated taking care of things. You refused to take the class hamster home that one time in fourth grade 'cause you said it had an evil nose."

I shuddered. "That thing was creepy. But that was then. I have a guinea pig now."

"You do? Since when?"

I just looked at him, and Kareem winced and fell silent.

"Anyway, that little alien is lost, hungry, and, from what I can tell, alone," I continued to say, ignoring Juan Carlos's loud wails and the weird smell coming from his foot. "I'm assuming it has no clue how to fix its ship on its own. Everything is different here. Cheese doesn't even have hands like we do! It can probably, like, move stuff with its mind where it's from! I'm not turning Cheese over to an *adult* just so they can lecture us and then turn our little alien over to some secret lab or something, then pretend everything is normal!"

"Yeah, this is definitely not normal," Kareem said, chewing his lip.

"No, it's not, and I'm cool with that. Normal is a lie. Normal means people keep stuff from you so everything looks okay, but just when you least expect it, *BAM!*, things get abnormal." I made a fist and punched my other hand, then frowned. That actually hurt.

Kareem sighed and shook his head. "You're abnormal," he muttered.

"Your face is abnormal."

He made a face and threw a clump of grass at me. I dodged and kicked a pebble at him, and he grinned. A smile started to cross my face, but just then Juan Carlos hobbled past, moaning like a zombie, smelling like dog poop, both hands covering his eyes.

"My *shooooooooooooooeeee*," he moaned. Kareem and I raised our eyebrows, then collapsed in laughter.

At that moment it felt like a huge weight had been lifted off my shoulders. Kareem and me, laughing together for the first time in months. It felt good. Odd, but good.

"It's not funny," Juan Carlos said as we held our sides and tears streamed down our faces. "Mami is gonna kill me!"

"I hope she washes you first," Kareem gasped.

"Dude, you smell like you've literally been kicking butt," I said, and Kareem howled with laughter. Juan Carlos glared at both of us, but then the corners of his mouth twitched and he shook his head and started laughing with us.

"You two are weird," he said.

We carried on like that down the street, sometimes jogging, sometimes staggering along like Juan Carlos, dragging our feet until they were clean, three poop zombies on the hunt for food.

Pink-tipped clouds covered the sky as the sun set on our East End neighborhood. It was still warm out, and I could tell this summer was going to be a doozy. Everybody else could, too. They gathered on the street corners or porches or leaned on fences, and it felt like the whole city scrunched together into our neighborhood. Four city blocks of family.

Before the factory closed, at the end of the workday people would come streaming out when the whistle sounded. It was like a walking block party for miles. Kids ran to their moms and dads. Store owners propped their doors open and called to friends and family. The neighborhood came alive at night, and no place symbolized that more than Jorge's Bodega.

Jorge was a balding, tall Latino man who had light brown skin and a laugh that sounded like a parrot squawk. You had to get used to it, because he found *everything* funny. I liked him. He always smiled, always had something nice to say, and always had snacks for a kid who might've missed lunch hiding from a bully.

"Ethan, my man!" Jorge called as we jogged up to the front of his bodega. Kareem was still in the back of the pack, slow as always. Jorge held a broom in one hand and a small towel in the other. He wiped his forehead and leaned on the end of the broom's handle. "What's the rush, man, you smell my quesadillas?" He slapped his knee and squawked his laugh.

"Hi, Mr. Jorge. *Um*, is my brother around?"

"I told him to cut out a little early," Jorge said, waving his hand. "Better things for a kid to be doing on a day like this than working."

Bummer. I was hoping to get Troy to sneak me some food for the . . .

"Visitor?" Jorge said. I almost jumped, thinking he was reading my mind and seeing the alien. But he was nodding at Juan Carlos. "I don't think I've seen him around."

"This is Juan Carlos," I said, waving my new neighbor forward.

Jorge looked down at Juan's dirty shirt and crumpled-up shoe. "I swear, Ethan, you find the most Ethan-y friends."

"Thanks," I said, unsure if that was a compliment or not.

"So, what's up?"

"Just some snacks!" Kareem yelled as he finally caught up.

Jorge looked past me. "Kareem? Is that you? I haven't seen you in months!"

Kareem smiled as he dapped Jorge up.

"I know, man. We moved."

"How's your parents doing?"

Kareem's eyes shifted as he backed away from Jorge. "They're fine," Kareem said quickly, then he zipped into the bodega.

"What's the matter with Kareem's parents?" I asked when Kareem was out of earshot.

Jorge frowned. "I don't know, *is* something wrong with his parents?" Jorge seemed confused by the question; but I had to remind myself, people don't see what I see. Jorge hadn't noticed Kareem's discomfort when he asked about his parents. But I had. Something was up.

What had happened to Kareem's family? Is that why he'd had to move? But why would he stop talking to me?

"Well, we'll be back. Going to get a few things," I said, and walked inside.

"Ethan," Juan Carlos shouted from an aisle, "he's got hot pickles!" He held up a large pickle floating in a water balloon–like bag of green pickle juice. He was now wearing his one dry sock on one foot and his one non-chewed shoe on the other foot.

"Remember, we're getting food for Cheese," I said, getting closer so Jorge couldn't overhear.

"What does an alien eat?" Kareem whispered.

I shrugged. "Just grab a bunch of stuff. It's gotta like *something*."

We busied ourselves grabbing different snacks. I kicked myself for leaving my book bag at the factory. I'd been so scared Cheese was going to eat one of us, I'd run off without it. Just then, a thought popped into my mind. *HANDY-BOT! What if Cheese eats Handy-Bot?*

"Guys, we have to hurry," I rushed.

"Okay, I've got an oatmeal creme pie, a bag of hot cheese puffs, and some beef jerky," Kareem announced.

"Umgudhootpeekles," Juan Carlos said.

Kareem and I stared at him.

He blushed, then swallowed the huge mouthful of hot pickle he'd been eating.

"Sorry. I said I got hot pickles." He went back to gnawing on the giant pickle. Green pickle juice splashed everywhere. *Yuck.*

"*Okaaay.* Well, I've got a chocolate bar, a can of biscuit dough, and a couple pouches of juice. I think we're set. How much money has each of you got?"

The fellas looked at me like *I* had suddenly become an alien.

"What, you thought I was paying for all this by myself?"

"Well, it *was* your idea," said Kareem.

"Come on, you guys. Imagine if you were alone, on a different planet, and hungry. How would you want to be greeted?"

"I feel that. Nobody even greeted me when I moved here," Juan said.

I looked at Juan, suddenly understanding what my mom had been trying to tell me.

"Cheese should feel welcomed. I'm in." Juan Carlos reached in his pocket to pull out a few bills.

"My allowance got cut," Kareem said.

I wasn't sure I could believe him, but I left it alone. Besides, me and Juan together covered the bill. We made our purchase, thanked Jorge, and after I grabbed a big handful of hot sauce packets—just in case—the three of us hurried back to the factory.

"Hey, what's that?" Juan Carlos asked. He pointed to a trio of cars parked down the street, lined in a row in front of a neighborhood barbershop. Two cops talked to Rick the Barber, and another took notes. Two people in gray suits, a man and a woman, stepped out of the barbershop, heads close like they were talking low.

I could feel Kareem tense up beside me at the sight of the cops. The police didn't have the greatest reputation in my neighborhood.

As we watched, the two people in gray suits seemed to finish talking, then one pulled out something that looked like a metal detector. They started waving it around Rick, who backed up, shaking his head. The two cops who had been questioning Rick grabbed him by the arms and held him tight while the suits continued to scan him. When he struggled, they shoved him against the wall. I squeezed my fists tight.

"Who are those people with the cops?" Juan asked me.

"I don't know," I answered. My heart had started to hammer. "I never seen 'em. Maybe FBI, CIA, MIB, MI6, no telling. I don't even want to know. Let's get out of here, that alien needs the food."

9

HOW TO FEED AN ALIEN!

Walking with junk food stuffed down your shirt and pants is the worst. I mean, the worst. Crinkly wrappers poke you and make you itch in places you probably shouldn't scratch in public. But we do what we have to, so aliens won't eat our clothes.

Kareem glanced at the sky nervously. The sun touched the horizon. The shadows started to stretch and creep around us. We all shuffled along the sidewalk, hoping no one stopped us. I hid my face as we passed my house and headed toward the fence at the end of the block. The lights were on, and I could hear Dad's favorite oldies station playing from the lone window in the attic.

"Maybe we should go back tomorrow," Kareem said, not looking at either Juan Carlos or myself. "I have to catch the bus all the way to the other side of town."

"You can leave if you want. You're good at that," I said.

Kareem frowned. "And let you get all the credit for this discovery? Not a chance. Just saying, it's getting dark."

He was right. Just like him, I had to be home by the time the streetlights came on.

"We won't be long. Twenty minutes, tops."

He opened his mouth to argue again, but I cut him off. "Basement Rule," I said.

His eyes widened. "Nah, that's not fair! That was a totally different situation!"

We had already made it past the fence, and now Juan Carlos looked at both of us, confused.

"What's a basement rule?" he asked.

"Not *a* basement rule, *the* Basement Rule. Why don't you tell him what that is, Kareem?"

I didn't know if that rule still meant anything to him. For a second I thought Kareem wouldn't say anything, but he began to speak after kicking at a loose rock.

"The Basement Rule means you can't let another person go somewhere creepy by themselves."

"And how did that start?" I asked.

He shot me a look. "You already know."

"Yeah, but Juan Carlos doesn't."

Kareem rolled his eyes and kicked at another rock. I wondered if he was imagining my face on the rocks as he kicked them.

Hmm.

That's a cool idea for an invention—a shoe projector that puts the faces of people who annoy you on rocks. Then, you can kick them without actually being sent to the principal's office. Nice.

"Fine," Kareem finally said. "Ethan came with me to get one of his super-Frisbees out of my basement one night. The electricity was out, and that rocket-powered Frisbee was the only thing that worked in the entire neighborhood."

"That doesn't sound bad," Juan Carlos said.

"You don't know his basement," I answered. "All basements are creepy by default. Fact. But his basement had these giant spiders and cobwebs that felt like fingers on your neck, and the pipes down there sounded like someone was rattling chains nearby, and this one time something moaned and—"

"Okay!" Kareem interrupted. "You don't have to make us relive it. Anyway, whenever one of us feels creeped out by a place, the Basement Rule means they don't have to go alone. Except in this case he's not alone, he has you."

Kareem pointed at Juan Carlos, who shook his head and took a step back.

"Uh-uh. I don't like basements either."

I picked up the pace. "See? We're all in this together. Now come on, before those oatmeal creme pies splatter everywhere."

"I also don't like cellars," Juan Carlos muttered. "Or stair-wells, or broom closets, or broom closets under stairwells, or . . ."

I shook my head as he continued talking and we made our way back to the greatest thing to hit this town since double chocolate chip cookies became free during our school lunch-time. And that was super cool.

We stepped inside the secret factory entrance and huddled around the door to the main floor. Juan Carlos stood behind Kareem, who stood behind me. I felt their eyes judging me as I hesitated.

"Come on, Ethan," Kareem said.

"Yeah, come on, Ethan," Juan Carlos repeated.

I glanced back at the two of them and made a rude gesture, but luckily and unluckily neither of them saw it.

Lucky, because I could feel my mother's "Ethan Alert" activating as soon as I made the gesture.

Unlucky, because the reason neither of them saw it was because the entire factory was completely dark, except for the moonlight that shone through the hole in the roof.

"The streetlights gotta be on," I said slowly, trying to back up, but Kareem nudged me forward.

"Nuh-uh, dude. You brought us here. You don't get to back out now."

Juan Carlos—at least, I thought it was Juan Carlos—moved to my other shoulder. I didn't want to reach out and try to see if it was him, but thankfully he chimed in with his own view of our current predicament.

"I should've stayed home with Abuela," he muttered. "I'd still have a good shoe, my foot wouldn't stink, my stomach wouldn't gurgle. . . ."

"Okay, we get it," I said.

Our whispers echoed around us. Okay, somebody had to do something. I took a deep breath and clutched the snacks even tighter, then stepped carefully out onto the factory floor. After a second or two, I heard the other two shuffling after me.

Again, I hoped it was them.

Have you ever had the lights go off suddenly right when you were in an unfamiliar place? Like your grandmother's kitchen, or in the locker room right as you're getting dressed? That's how it felt. The darkness hung all around us like inky black curtains. I couldn't see my hand even when I brought it right to my nose.

But that wasn't the worst part.

What *really* made things super creepy were all the sounds that seemed to get louder when you couldn't see what had made them.

Creaks.

Squeaks.

Scrapes.

Gurgles.

Wait: gurgles?

Oh, give me a break.

"Juan Carlos, seriously, eat another pickle if your stomach is rumbling that much," I whispered.

Something shuffled to my left.

"What are you talking about?" I heard Juan Carlos say. "That wasn't me."

Something shuffled again, and I felt something graze my arm.

"Cheese and crackers?!"

I screamed and jumped backward. Kareem grunted as I crashed into him, and Juan Carlos yelped as we all fell. We flailed in a pile of tangled arms, legs, and hot sauce packets.

I whipped out my flashlight. I probably should've turned it on much earlier, honestly.

Our intergalactic friend stood in front of us. I could almost read the pleased expression on its silver face.

"Jeez, Cheese," I said before I could stop myself. Someone squirmed beneath me.

"Cudjapweezgedduhp?" I heard somebody say.

"Oh, sorry."

I rolled off the pile and got up. Kareem rubbed his nose as he got to his feet, then helped Juan Carlos off the floor. Our snacks lay scattered on the ground, but right now all eyes were on Cheese as it hovered this way and that.

When Cheese finally landed, the armlike appendage extended and poked at the snacks, gentle at first, then more eagerly when they didn't explode.

Hmm.

Exploding oatmeal creme pies.

You know . . .

Wait, I had to focus.

I groped through the dark to find my backpack, then pulled out a power pack. I always keep a flashlight in my backpack, but the power pack makes it way brighter. It was like having a floodlight in the factory.

I turned back just as Cheese picked up a treat and zipped it into its mouth. It did the alien version of chewing, which I guess meant wobbling back and forth and spinning; and then it zoomed around the room, chirping excitedly.

"Cheese and crackers! Cheese and crackers!"

"I guess it likes oatmeal creme pies," Kareem said. He pulled another off the floor and opened it, then tossed it at Cheese. The alien snatched it out of the air and gobbled it up. Then it looked at all of us and said something in its alien language. I glanced at Kareem and Juan Carlos and shrugged.

"It likes them."

Cheese chirped something else and bobbed expectantly. I got the feeling it was sad. Like, it wanted more.

"Cheese is still hungry, guys," I said. I started to grab a bag of hot cheese puffs when Juan Carlos grabbed my wrist.

"Wait!" he said excitedly. "That's it!"

"What's it?" Kareem asked, but Juan Carlos had already dropped to the floor and started gathering up armfuls of snacks.

He held up a bag of chips. Cheese stared. Juan tossed the chips to the side and held up a chocolate bar. Still Cheese did nothing.

Then Juan Carlos pulled a pickle from the pile. He held it up, and the alien froze. I mean, it didn't bob, twirl, spin, or anything. Its large eyes lasered in on that pickle, and I tensed up. What if pickles were some deadly insult to Cheese's species? Like, you pulled out a pickle when you were about to fight. Or what if pickles were like mosquitoes on its planet?

But then Cheese twirled and bobbed excitedly.

"That's it. When he spins, it must mean yes."

It was an interesting observation. I can't say I wasn't impressed. "You're right, toss him the pickle."

Juan tossed Cheese the pickle and the alien trembled with excitement as it caught it and shoved it into its mouth. If I didn't know better, I would have said that Cheese liked them almost as much as Juan Carlos did. Maybe more. The only thing Cheese seemed to like even *better* was the hot sauce packets, which the guys and I took turns opening and squeezing into the alien's mouth.

"I wonder what other foods it would like," Kareem said, smiling affectionately. "Maybe it would like pancakes, or veggie burgers. Ooh, what about pigs in a blanket?"

"I bet it would," Juan Carlos said.

"Or lasagna. Or mashed potatoes."

"Yeah, but we should—"

"Or chicken nommies!"

Juan Carlos and I stared at Kareem. Excitement slowly faded to embarrassment and he cleared his throat. "*Ahem.* I mean chicken nuggets. Only little kids and babies eat chicken nommies. I don't even know what those are."

Juan Carlos looked at him suspiciously. "Riiight. Anyway, we know what *yes* is for Cheese. Now we should try some other words."

"Like 'poop foot,'" Kareem said, waving a hand in front of his nose. "Seriously, bro, your foot still stinks. Can't you scrub it with some dirt or something? You're setting a bad example for our guest from beyond the stars. What if it thinks all humans have one foot that smells like poop?"

"What if it thinks all humans eat chicken nommies?" Juan Carlos shot back.

The two started arguing about which first impression was worse. I sighed and tossed Cheese another pickle. We kept feeding Cheese, and the more it ate, the smoother its skin became, and the dark spots began to disappear until there were none left. It was working! Then something incredible happened. Cheese shot up into the air, floating about the room, twirling and speaking in its high-pitched voice. It was obviously happy and had regained its energy.

"Is that the only hand it has?" Juan Carlos asked when Cheese used the silver arm to eat something else.

"I think so."

"Must be tough," Juan Carlos said, chewing his pickle. "I wonder if on its planet there's gravity like ours. I bet everything is super heavy here to Cheese."

"All the more reason we need to help it," Kareem said. That made me feel good. Someone else understood why we couldn't just leave Cheese alone.

I took out another pickle, took a small nibble, then shrugged. These things *were* pretty good.

CHEESE HAS A MAJOR PROBLEM

While Kareem and Juan Carlos played with Cheese, I decided to investigate Cheese's ship. I'd stopped myself before, out of fear of offending or angering Cheese—and also just out of plain fear. But now that we seemed to be buddies, maybe I could take a peek. A quick look. Nothing more.

I grabbed my sketchbook and tiptoed over to where the spacecraft was, ready to take notes and learn about the ship our new friend had arrived in.

Observation number one: the spaceship was bigger than before. Even though it was metal, it appeared to have expanded.

Observation number two: the spacecraft's surface was so smooth and silver, it was reflective. The ship looked like a giant pinball. Even when you touched it, you didn't leave fingerprints.

Observation number three: Cheese had entered the ship through a door. How had he activated it? That was more of a question, but I thought it needed to be asked.

The ship was amazing. I reached out and ran my fingers across the smooth metal surface. It was cool to the touch. I could see scratches and dents on the exterior. The ship had had a tough landing. Every spot I touched glowed faintly, much dimmer than the day before. The ship was losing power.

A loud chirp of surprise echoed around the warehouse. I turned to find Cheese standing behind me, spinning and wobbling in distress. The alien chirped something else, and I backed up, suddenly cautious.

"Okay, okay, I'm sorry," I said. "I just wanted to take a look."

Cheese calmed down as I backed up. It didn't like me going near the ship.

All of a sudden, things began to make sense.

An alien hiding in a factory. The fresh hole in the ceiling.

"You didn't land here," I said. "You *crashed* here, didn't you?"

Kareem and Juan Carlos walked up as I paced back and forth, trying to put the clues together in a way that made sense. Sometimes genius inventors had to become genius detectives.

"There's something wrong with your spaceship, isn't there? You need help repairing it, don't you?"

Juan looked confused. "How'd you figure that?"

"Look." I pointed at a dim section of the ship. "I think the ship glows when it turns on and is working properly. Right now it's almost completely dark. Yesterday it was glowing more. I think it's getting worse."

"You think you can fix it?" Juan Carlos asked, skeptical. To be honest, I didn't know if I could. I'd started to shrug when Kareem interrupted.

"Of course, he can," Kareem mumbled.

Kareem kicked at something on the floor and didn't meet my eyes.

I didn't know what to say, but it felt good to hear him say that. I felt a boost of confidence lift my spirits, and I grinned. "I can't do it without you, though."

I looked at Juan. "You too, bro. You're a part of the team now."

Something brushed past my legs and I jumped in surprise. I sighed when I saw the alien's silver arm sneaking along the floor to get another pickle. Some people are just plain greedy. Or aliens. Some aliens are just plain greedy.

I cleared my throat. "First things first. We can't fix anything if we don't know what's wrong. And Cheese won't let me get close."

"Maybe we smell," Juan Carlos said. Kareem and I just looked at him. Juan Carlos hung his head. "I mean, maybe *I* smell."

Kareem patted his back in sympathy.

"Well, I don't think it's the poop foot," I said. "I think Cheese is worried we'll break it even more."

"Well," Juan Carlos said, thinking. "What if we show it how good you are at fixing things?"

"What do you mean?" I asked.

"Maybe Cheese thinks we might break something. The ship's already busted. Show it something you've built."

I slapped my head. "Juan Carlos, you're a genius!" Juan gave a smile. "Kareem, can you wheel in Handy-Bot? Let's give Cheese a demonstration."

Kareem nodded, immediately understanding. "You got it!"

Cheese looked curious and hovered around us as we set up our demonstration and came up with a rough script. The pickle supply was almost out, but that was cool, because apparently it was in the mood to try out the super-hot cheese puffs too.

I stepped back. "All right, I think we're ready. Everybody knows what to do?"

Kareem and Juan Carlos nodded.

Cheese burped.

At least I hoped it was a burp.

"Good. All right, here we go."

I turned around and opened my sketchbook. A pencil rolled out. I grabbed it and began to sketch. The plan didn't call for me to draw anything specific, so I just started sketching the Pinball. Meanwhile, Juan Carlos started to talk really loudly to Kareem.

"OH, HI, KAREEM," he shouted. "I DIDN'T SEE YOU. I WAS JUST WORKING ON MY ROBOT."

Why is he so loud?

Kareem must've wondered the same thing. He plugged his ears and said the lines we'd worked on.

"Oh, wow, that's a nice robot Juan Carlos. How does it work?"

"I'M SO HAPPY YOU ASKED!"

Juan Carlos pushed Handy-Bot forward. Cheese paused as it ate another bag of cheese puffs—and I do mean a bag. Juan Carlos flipped the switch, and then, before anything happened, threw his hands up in horror.

"OH, NO! MY ROBOT!"

Several seconds of silence passed. I squirmed in embarrassment. Luckily, our audience didn't seem to care. Cheese stared at the robot, snacks forgotten. Finally, Kareem nudged Handy-Bot with his foot, and the robot rumbled to life.

I'd loosened one of Handy-Bot's arms, and as the robot began to run through its warm-up routine, the stretchy tube fell off with a clunk. Dust started spraying everywhere, and Kareem and Juan Carlos pretended to be upset. Well, Kareem started to pretend, but then he yelped when something got into his eye. Maybe I should've dumped those vacuum tanks.

"WHAT SHOULD I DO?" Juan Carlos yelled above the noise.

I leaped to my feet and rushed over. "I can help!" I shut off the switch, then picked up the arm and held it up. "Here's your problem! This robot lost its arm!"

Look, I never claimed to be a genius at acting or directing.

Anyway, it seemed to be working. Cheese floated closer and bobbed in concern. I didn't look at the alien, but I held up the arm so everyone could see it. Then I rubbed my chin and made a big show of walking around Handy-Bot. I knew how to fix it. I had one of the loose screws in my pocket. But if this was going to work, it had to look difficult.

"I don't know," I said, milking the suspense.

"WHAT DO YOU MEAN—"

I glared at Juan Carlos.

"—you don't know?" he finished in a whisper.

"This looks tough," I said. Then, with what I hoped was a subtle motion, I coughed and pulled the screw out of my pocket. I glanced at Cheese, and he didn't seem to have noticed. I dropped to a knee, whipped out a screwdriver, and soon Handy-Bot was back to normal.

"There. Fixed. Give it a go, buddy."

Juan Carlos flipped the switch, and a much quieter robot powered up.

"Handy-Bot, clean," Juan Carlos said.

I watched with pride as the robot I'd designed zipped into action. Handy-Bot dashed around the room, cleaning and scrubbing the floor. Cheese looked amazed. A half-eaten bag of hot cheese puffs dangled from its mouth as it hovered behind Handy-Bot. Cheese peered at the spinning brush and even used its lone arm to lift the "repaired" arm.

If I hadn't known better, I'd have said that was one wowed alien.

Cheese chirped something and looked at me.

"Yep. All fixed. If that's what you're asking."

Cheese turned back to the robot and lifted the arm again. Handy-Bot idled with a soft hum, waiting for the next instruction. Cheese moved around it, examining every feature and modification. Kareem and I exchanged nervous glances.

Juan Carlos seemed happy with his role. He stood off to the side, practicing his lines as if we were going to do the whole thing over.

"OH no my robot. Oh NO my ROBOT. Oh no my ro-BOT!"

I shook my head.

Cheese chirped again and headed toward us. It didn't bob or twirl or grab any snacks as it passed. I cleared my throat. The alien turned to me and stared with wide dark eyes. I decided talking wasn't necessary right now. Cheese paused at the Pinball, then chirped once in a clear tone.

"What's he doing?" Kareem whispered.

"*Shh*," I said.

"Is it singing?" Juan Carlos asked.

"*Shhhhh*," I said again, trying to focus on the alien and how it interacted with its ship. The giant spacecraft now pulsed with a soft, golden light. As Cheese chirped, the lights responded.

"It's like a code." Kareem raised an eyebrow, and I realized I'd spoken aloud. "It's like the voice activation for Handy-Bot. The ship is responding to Cheese's voice."

Cheese spoke and, sure enough, the door of the ship opened. Cheese floated into the ship, then turned and chirped at me.

"I think it wants you to go with him," Kareem whispered.

"Our plan worked!" Juan Carlos said with hushed excitement.

A feeling of nervous energy spread up and down my spine. This was it. Cheese bobbed up and down and chirped again, urgently.

"Coming," I called out. Then, with slow, cautious steps, I walked up to the Pinball.

11

AN INVENTOR'S DREAM

A while ago, back when Kareem and I still rode the dingy yellow school bus every morning and everything made sense, our fifth-grade class took a trip to the Ferrous City Indoor Botanical Gardens.

We spent the bus ride cracking jokes and trading role-playing game cards. Somebody brought a mini speaker, and the chaperones let us play songs for most of the trip, until somebody slipped in one with lyrics that made everybody freeze. Our teacher, Mrs. Washington, leaped out of her seat like something bit her butt and stomped down the aisle to confiscate the speaker.

We pulled up to our destination sulking and angry. But when the class filed out and marched inside, we promptly forgot about the bus ride.

The Gardens turned a rowdy bunch of preteens into an awestruck group of students. Amazement hid around every corner. Giant leafy plants that smelled like cinnamon, flowering bushes, and humongous trees that stretched to the greenhouse ceiling. We *oohed* and *aahed* for the entire ninety minutes.

But the thing that I remember most was the giant indoor pond filled with floating flowers. No two flowers were the same. Some were big with drooping petals, some were tiny with sharp thorns. Some were purple, some were blue, some were a combination of pink and white and this sort of blurry orange.

I stood at that pond for the whole trip, amazed at the combination of colors and scents, determined to fix that moment in my mind, because I was sure I'd never experience something so beautiful and rare again in my life. Not in Ferrous City.

I was wrong.

"Cheese. And. Crackers." The inside of Cheese's ship was unlike anything I had ever seen. When I walked through the door, a ramp led up to the platform of the ship where there was a golden glow.

When I got to the platform, the first thing that struck me was the fact that I could see clear through the walls!

Observation number four: somehow the metal exterior was transparent from the inside of the ship. I didn't know how to explain it.

I peered out of the ship right at Juan Carlos and Kareem, but they couldn't see me. Kareem was checking his teeth in the reflection of the ship. Good thing, too, 'cause there was stuff all in there. On the other side of the ship, I saw Juan pick a booger and sniff it. The things we do when we think nobody's watching.

I walked over to touch the wall, but my foot slipped into some sort of gutter covered in golden dust. The dust glowed so brightly, it lit up the whole ship. I followed the gutter with my eyes; it wrapped all the way around the ship, clear to the other side. I stepped back onto the platform and brushed myself off.

The inside of the ship was pretty much empty, other than the control center at the front end—or back end, I'm not really sure. There were broken flowers thrown all about the ship. I hesitate to call them flowers because they were metal, just like the exterior of the ship. Some of the flowers remained intact and glowed faintly, but most were crushed and dark.

I sniffed the air. "Is that vanilla? And cinnamon?" The sweet and spicy aroma made my eyes close and my mouth water. It smelled like fresh-baked cookies cooling in a kitchen.

Cheese chirped at me and I got the feeling it wanted me to walk deeper into the ship. It wasn't like I was scared or anything. Still, I hesitated.

The alien chirped something impatiently. I flapped a hand and took my sweet time gathering myself. "Yeah, yeah," I said. "Gimme a moment."

I took a few more steps. Even though the floor looked like metal, it felt spongy.

I've never seen metal like this.

I could tell the inside used to be a pristine white, but the golden dust was splattered all across the ship—from the crash, I was sure. I started to wonder if the dust and broken flowers were connected.

Cheese floated by a giant cracked display screen at the control panel and fiddled with it. The control panel was a small desk-like platform. There was a screen in the middle, sort of like an interface. I imagined it did all the things you needed to operate the ship. On either side of the screen were three circular silver objects that looked like dinner plates. Connected to each plate was a different-colored metal flower that glowed brightly. One was gold like the dust in the gutter of the ship. *Ah-ha!* I thought. The dust *did* come from the flowers, like some sort of pollen.

Cheese chirped softly, but it still didn't look at me. It moved to one of the flowers near the control panel. Its arm shot out to spin the flower. The dust from the flower whirled and spun to form images and pictures, like a glowing slideshow.

It showed Cheese's ship, cruising through space.

"Oh, cool, that's you," I said excitedly.

But all of a sudden Cheese's ship started to fall, faster and faster; and pretty soon, the ship was barreling toward Earth.

Cheese seemed to hover lower and lower until he nearly touched the floor.

I stood there, confused. Something had obviously happened while Cheese was piloting this ship, and he'd crashed here on Earth. Now Cheese was stuck here, and the poor creature looked heartbroken. I couldn't speak its language, but I knew when someone was bummed out.

That was me after Kareem left.

I gave the alien a minute to pull itself together. I took some scrap paper and a broken pencil out of my book bag and began sketching the control room. Good inventors always record their observations.

"Amazing," I whispered, leaning in close.

My pencil fell out of my hand and clattered on one of the plates. I looked around, but Cheese didn't seem to notice. I reached down to grab the pencil. My hand brushed a flower. The metal petals shook, then opened like a rose blooming in the morning.

"Cheese and crackers!"

The glowing pollen inside shot out, and another short movie played. A twirling and bobbing alien hovered above the plate before bursting into a cloud of silver dust that floated back down into the flower. The petals curled back up and closed tight.

"Cheese, was that you!?"

I turned and scanned the room, but Cheese had disappeared. I activated Cheese's flower again and laughed at his display. The goofy alien was wiggling and shaking its butt in the air.

"Nice moves, dude."

But this time Cheese's display played longer. Four other aliens appeared and tossed Cheese in the air. It looked surprised, but the others caught it and gathered around, and soon all five bobbed and twirled together. Cheese seemed to be the baby of the group.

"Cheese, is that your family?" I asked.

Silence.

Cheese still hadn't reappeared. "Now where did it go?"

Something dinged. I ignored it, but then it started dinging again and again. I looked around in confusion. The sound was coming from my wrist. My heart started pounding.

"Oh no. Oh no, no, no. Oh no-no-no-no-no-no-no!"

I checked my watch, the alarm on it still sounding as the little light flashed on and off.

I was so dead.

"Streetlights!"

I silenced the alarm. I hesitated, then grabbed one of Cheese's metal flower displays and shoved it in my pocket. I just hoped I wouldn't start trailing gold dust when I ran home.

If my Mom would still *let* me come home!

Streetlight-rule violations were serious business. Maybe if they bought me another phone, I could call. But I knew what they'd say: *We bought you a phone that you tried to turn into an underwater call interceptor. You can have another phone when you're fifteen.*

So unfair.

I whirled around, but Cheese was still missing. I scrambled across the ship and climbed out. Kareem and Juan Carlos stood nervously.

"Dude, we were worried sick!" Kareem shouted.

Juan Carlos patted me all over. "You got all your arms and legs? Show me your fingers and toes. Show me the toes, Ethan!"

I slapped his hands away and grabbed them both by the shoulder and said one word.

"Streetlights."

Kareem's eyes widened.

Juan Carlos's jaw dropped.

"We are—" Kareem said.

"—so dead," Juan Carlos finished.

"Wait," I cried, as they both made to sprint off. "We can't just leave the Pinball like this. What if somebody comes in here? What if they find it, or Cheese?"

"Man, nobody comes in here!" Kareem said, trying to urge me toward the door.

"Just in case!" I cried. "Remember, if we're the discoverers, we don't want somebody else to take the credit! Right?"

Juan Carlos and Kareem hesitated, then quickly walked back.

"Okay, but where?"

"I know the perfect spot," I said, relieved that they were going to help. I wasn't sure if I'd be able to move the Pinball without them.

As it turned out, it was extremely easy to move, and I *could've* done it by myself. Whatever it was made of, it was light as a feather, even if it didn't look like it. We guided it to the hiding spot—an opening in a brick wall with some old factory machine that appeared to block the entrance. I'd explored this place from floor to ceiling and had missed this at first. On first and even second glance, it just looked like the machine took up the whole space. But behind the metal frame was a big empty area that used to be a storeroom, I think. It was the perfect spot for the Pinball. If anyone looked here, they would think the spaceship was part of the old factory equipment. Perfect.

I wondered if there was some kind of cloaking device Cheese could activate for the Pinball. But even if I could speak its language to ask, Cheese was still nowhere to be found. I paused, searching with my eyes, but Kareem and Juan Carlos nudged me.

"Come *on*, Ethan!"

I nodded, and without another word grabbed my backpack and slung it over my shoulder. It was heavier than I remembered. I had way too much junk in there. I glanced around. Handy-Bot would have to stay here. There was no way I could make it home quickly enough to avoid a major punishment lugging that thing behind me.

"Let's go, dude," Kareem shouted. He pulled out the remaining snacks in his pocket and laid them on the floor, then he and Juan Carlos sprinted for the door to the secret entrance. I glanced back, hoping to catch a glimpse of Cheese so I could tell the alien goodbye. Nothing.

"'Bye, buddy," I said softly.

Then I took off, sprinting like mad, hoping I wouldn't be grounded until I turned thirty.

12

INSERT FOOT IN MOUTH

The streetlights hummed beneath the evening sky. A few hadn't flickered on yet, and I prayed to whoever watched over genius inventors that the lights on our block were still off.

"If I miss my bus, my dad is gonna kill me," Kareem panted as we scrambled over the fence.

"Yours? Mine is gonna kill me, tell the doctors to bring me back to life, then kill me again!" I was exaggerating, but the punishment it looked like I was destined to receive loomed over me like the moon peeking out from behind the clouds.

Juan Carlos had a scared expression on his face. Or maybe sad. I couldn't tell, but he was certainly feeling something.

"Is your grandma going to punish you?" I asked.

He looked at me with big, wide eyes. "I never told her about my shoe," he whispered. "That was my school shoe."

Both Kareem and I flinched. Shoes got messed up all the time—scuffs, stains, even losing shoelaces when they were needed to tie a robot's eyes in place. But school shoes . . . those were never to be worn outside of school for any reason AT ALL. Sometimes Mom would make me take my beat-up sneakers just so I could put them on before I stepped out the school doors. And now Juan Carlos had ruined his. Well, an alien ate it, but who'd believe that?

I felt bad for the kid. I felt like I was the cause.

"I'm sorry, man," I told him. "Maybe you can blame it on me, if that'll help."

"Yeah, maybe," he said as he trudged along.

We cut through someone's backyard. Kareem slowed down.

"What are you doing?" I asked.

"We're already late," he said. "Why race home, just to be punished earlier?"

That actually made sense. Juan Carlos and I slowed to a fast walk, and I shoved my hands in my pockets. The metal flower I'd taken felt cool, and it reminded me of Cheese's problems.

"At least we all have family we can go home to," I said quietly.

Kareem scoffed. "What's that supposed to mean?"

I shrugged. "Some people, or aliens, don't have what you have."

"Shut up," Kareem whispered.

I whipped around, shocked. Juan Carlos frowned.

"What?" I said.

"Shut! Up! You don't know anything!"

Kareem started walking diagonally across the street, away from both of us. Juan Carlos raised his hands in confusion, and I gawked.

I'd never seen Kareem act like that.

Juan Carlos glanced at me, eyebrow raised. "Is he okay?"

I shrugged, not really sure what to say. "I guess I should go find out."

"Yeah, you should," he said. "I'm headed home."

I nodded and we gave each other dap. I watched him head into his house on the corner. Then I turned and jogged to catch up to Kareem, who was still walking away.

"Hey. Hey!" I caught up and started walking beside him. He didn't slow down, so I sort of jog-walked to keep his pace. "What was that about?"

"Nothing."

"That wasn't nothing. That was something. You just snapped on me for no reason."

"I said it was nothing, man. Leave me alone."

"Kareem—"

"Leave me alone!"

He pushed both hands into his pockets, hunched over, and walked faster. I stopped, watching him stalk off, trying to figure out what was eating him. Maybe he needed space. Maybe he needed some time to himself to deal with whatever had upset him. I don't know what I'd said, or what Juan Carlos had said, or what he thought we'd said, but he looked mad enough to kick boulders.

I could've just let him walk into the night. He wasn't my best friend anymore, anyway.

Right?

Who cares?

Let him go.

I turned and started to cross to my side of the street, heading to my house. Kareem reached the other side and headed to his bus stop, neither of us looking at the /other.

Who was he, to drop in and out of my life like that? Like he could pick up our friendship whenever he wanted or disappear when he felt like it? Who did that? Friends didn't do that. I wouldn't do that. I didn't do that.

This was all on him.

Yeah.

The more I thought about it, the angrier I got. Like really angry. Angry enough to shout something I probably shouldn't. But who cares?

I turned to yell something at my ex-best friend, then stopped.

Kareem had stopped walking, and his shoulders were shaking.

"Kareem?"

He didn't answer. I looked both ways, then jogged across the street.

"Kareem?"

He looked at me with wet, red eyes, and I didn't know what to do. He sniffled. Kareem *never* cried. Ever. I can count on one finger the number of times I saw him cry, and that was the time he broke his leg in kindergarten.

"Hey . . ." I stopped. What do you say to someone who's crying? "Are you okay? What's wrong, dude?"

Silence. Then: "I'm not supposed to talk about it with people."

Okaaay.

"Yo, if somebody's messing with you, we can go tell my—"

"No."

He took a deep breath, one of those ragged inhales that people do to try and suck in all the bad and exhale it all at once. When he let it out, he squared his shoulders and turned so he kind of faced me but didn't. He looked over my shoulder at something in the distance.

"I'm not supposed to tell you, or anyone, that my parents got a divorce," he whispered.

"Oh." It was a weak response, but I didn't know what to say.

"They asked me who I wanted to go with, and I went with my dad. That's why we moved. My mom left the city."

Kareem's tears started to flow. Everything he had been holding in, it all started to make sense why his behavior had changed so drastically. I couldn't imagine my family being broken up and what that might do to a kid.

Kareem looked at me, and I could see the hurt in his eyes.

He waited for something from me, and I knew I needed to say something, anything, but my mind was blank. What did words do, and how did I use them right now? They don't teach sixth-graders this stuff!

"Why didn't you just tell me, instead of acting weird?" It's not what I meant to say, but I guess, deep down, I was thinking it.

"It's always about you, isn't it, Ethan?" He bit his lip and walked off.

My thoughts tripped over themselves as I walked the last dozen or so yards to my house. His words kept playing in my head: *My parents got a divorce. It's always about you, isn't it, Ethan?*

A few years ago on Halloween, Mom and Dad both had to work late, so they let me go trick-or-treating with Kareem and his family. Now, I love my mom and dad, but being with Kareem's family was the most fun I had ever had trick-or-treating. His parents were a little younger than mine and always had fun. When we went out that year, they dressed up as Mr. and Mrs. Frankenstein and KILLED it. Showed us up, honestly. They were like big kids, and it's something I always appreciated about his folks.

They would host cookouts and take Kareem and me to the mall. The last few months had been so weird to me because

Kareem didn't so much as call. He didn't return my messages, and he didn't say 'bye when they moved away. Now I realize he didn't have a chance to. He was dealing with his own pain, and I was being selfish.

I thought about the time Kareem and I had won that science fair. His parents had been the ones who took our photo.

I smiled at the memory.

Now they were divorced.

My smile disappeared.

I walked up to my house, so lost in thought that I bumped into someone standing on my porch steps.

"C'mon—" I began, thinking it might be one of my brothers, but I froze at the black leather utility belt around the blue uniform, the unmistakable black holster of a pistol sticking out, the hand that dropped to it by reflex, and I looked up into the face of a police officer.

"Excuse me, son," he said, politely but not friendly. I stepped carefully around him to where Mom and Dad stood in the doorway. The cop looked me up and down. I got this a lot. Being tall for your age makes people unsure if you're an adult or a child, and I guess the cop didn't know whether he had to worry or not.

Another cop looked over from next door, ready to hustle over, but when nothing happened he resumed talking to the neighbors through the screen door.

Mom and Dad both wore guarded expressions, like some-body wanted them to do something and they weren't quite sure what it was yet.

"Mom," I began, ready to apologize for being late, but she didn't even look at me.

"Go on inside, Ethan," she said.

"I just wanted to say I'm—"

"Inside, Ethan," Dad said. He did look at me, and he looked angry. At first I thought he was angry at me, but then he turned the look on the cop.

"Actually, I'd like to ask your son a few questions," the cop said.

"He's got nothing to say," Mom snapped.

The cop dropped the smile. "Ma'am, we have to ask these questions. I understand it's late, but we can do it now, or I can come back later with a warrant."

"For what?" my dad asked.

"We've been told there may be someone in this neighbor-hood harboring a wanted fugitive. We've been instructed to report any unusual or suspicious activity."

"That's ridiculous," my dad replied.

The cop sighed. "It's over my head, sir." Dad could tell the officer was just doing his job. We all could.

Dad unfolded his arms and Mom placed a hand on his shoulder without even looking at him. I still didn't know what was going on, but they did that silent parent communication thing, and then Dad's shoulders relaxed. The cop looked between them, then turned and studied me.

"Young man, have you or any of your friends seen anything out of the ordinary? Or new faces around?"

My fingers twitched toward the metal flower in my pocket. *Cheese.*

They had to be looking for Cheese.

"Out of the ordinary?" I asked, trying to stall for time. A plain black car pulled around the corner of my block and eased to a stop at the curb across the street. It was them again: the people I'd seen wanding Rick the Barber got out of the back seat. They wore those same bulky gray-pinstriped suits as they moved stiffly down the sidewalk.

"Son?"

The cop leaned forward, and I felt Dad place a hand on my shoulder.

"Have you seen anything?" the cop asked again.

The two suits across the street began walking up the block, talking with the cops. They seemed to be telling the police officers what to do.

"Young man, if you've seen anything—"

"He doesn't know anything," Mom interrupted. She stood firm, one hand on her hip and the other reaching out to grab my shoulder. "You're scaring him."

As the suits headed toward Mrs. McGee's porch, one of them caught me staring. I quickly turned away. I wasn't sure if I had brought attention to myself, but I had to get off this porch because I knew exactly who that fugitive was.

They *were* after Cheese.

"I did see some new people," I blurted out.

Everybody stopped and turned to look at me. The cop flashed a triumphant smirk at Mom, then pulled out a pen and pad.

"Go ahead, son. Tell me what you saw."

I licked my lips. "Me and my friends went to get some snacks from Jorge's Bodega, and these people we'd never seen before were standing around Rick's Barbershop. They roughed up Mr. Rick. Threw him against the wall."

Mom held her hand over her mouth. "Rick? Did someone hurt that poor old man?"

I nodded, then pointed at the duo across the street. "That's them right there."

The cop's friendly expression turned ugly. "They're with us," he said. "A special unit from out of town."

He glanced over his shoulder, then stood and stuffed the pen and pad back into his pocket. His partner walked down the steps at the house next door and shook his head and went around to the driver's side of the patrol car.

"Will that be all, officer?" Dad asked in a tone that meant that had better be all.

The cop glanced at him, Mom, then me. His eyes lingered on me, then he put his cap back on and turned and walked away without another word. He crossed the street and held a whispered conversation with the weird duo, then they all moved to the car.

We watched them get in their car and drive off. Mom's arm joined Dad's hand to slip around my shoulder.

"You did good, baby," she said, kissing the top of my head. "But don't think you're slick. We'll talk about you breaking streetlight curfew later. Now get inside and wash up for dinner."

I trudged inside. *I can't win.*

THE TALK

Nobody really talked during dinner. Dad had used the rest of his marinade to roast chicken and propped it up on creamy rice. It was delicious. I busied myself shoveling the meal into my mouth.

Chris, the third-youngest and my older brother by a year, scraped his plate clean and went to stand up.

"Hold on, Chris," Dad said. He set his fork and knife down and wiped his mouth with a napkin. "Your mother and I need to talk to you."

"To me?" Chris asked, his voice squeaking.

"To all of you," Mom said, looking around. Ant and Troy exchanged a glance, like they knew what was coming.

Dad nodded. "The twins have already had the talk, but we felt it was time you and Ethan got it as well."

"The talk?" I asked, my neck growing warm. "Dad, they give that in middle school now. The principal and the gym teacher give it, actually. It's called 'Growth and Development,' and they have this weird movie from 2002 or something and this boy and girl—"

"Ethan Edgar," Mom cut me off as Ant and Troy burst into laughter. Even Dad covered his mouth with his napkin and hid a smile. Mom glared at him, and he quickly turned it into a cough.

"Not *that* talk, son," he said, "although I've seen some of the looks you've been getting around the neighborhood. It might not be a bad idea to just sit down and go over—"

"No, Dad! I'm good, seriously," I quickly said, hiding my face in my hands.

Mom gave Dad a light shove. "Stop embarrassing him. And be serious."

Dad smiled at her, then he sighed and turned to us.

"Not *that* talk," he said again, "but the talk about how to interact with the police."

Oh. That *talk.*

"As Black people, we've got to be careful. Period. We're starting from behind in the race. The other team started off with two touchdowns already on the board, but we're starting from behind. So now you've got to fight twice as hard just to pull even. You understand?"

Chris nodded, while I frowned. Mom leaned over and put her hand on mine.

"You have to be twice as good to get half as far, baby. That's what my mother told me, and her mother told her."

"But that's not fair," I protested.

"Nobody said it was," Ant said, sipping his lemonade.

"Life ain't fair," Troy said.

"It isn't," Dad agreed. "But if I spent all my time complaining about how everything in life was stacked against us, I'd be talking till morning. The factory shutting down wasn't fair, but we dealt with it and moved on, right?"

I nodded slowly.

"Well, one of the things you need to understand, and quickly, is that people expect certain things from you. Because of the color of your skin. And not all of them are good."

"Like what?"

"They expect you to be less educated. They expect you to be a troublemaker."

"Good at sports," Troy added.

"But I suck at sports."

"Language, Ethan," Mom said softly.

"I mean, I'm not good at sports. I don't even like sports."

"The people who know you, know that. But those that don't are often inclined to believe whatever they've been told to believe. And they don't look for the good, they look for what they expect to see. Our history, Black history, is filled with incidents where that belief has been at the expense of our feelings, our money, and sometimes our lives."

"So what do I say to make people believe in who I am, not what they expect to see?" I asked.

Dad sat back and rubbed his head. "It's not your job to tell them to believe you. Your actions will speak louder than your words ever can."

Mom patted my arm and then leaned in to Dad. "Be Ethan, baby, and everyone will know you for the smart, super-inventor, beautiful brown boy your father and I raised."

Chris twisted his lips. "But what does this have to do with the police?"

Dad looked at the ceiling for a moment. Then he stood up and walked to the stove. Mom's eyes filled with worry. Dad liked to cook when he was stressed, and, sure enough, he pulled some bananas down from the rack and started peeling them.

"When I was a boy, my daddy sat me down and read to me from a handwritten list. It was something his dad, your great-grandfather, had written down for him. I've got it some-where upstairs in an old lockbox, but it was basically a set of rules for dealing with the police. Now it's been updated a few times. You don't really see too many cops on horseback any-more, for example. But the main points are the same.

"Rule one: Keep your hands where they can see them. Don't know how many times I've seen a man or woman get wrestled to the ground and a knee in the back just for fishing some gum out their pocket."

In my mind, I saw Rick the Barber shoved up against the brick wall, the cops surrounding him.

Ant spoke up. "Rule two: Don't run."

"Rule three: Be polite, same as with anyone else you were speaking with," Mom said.

"Rule four: Stay calm. Getting angry just gets people riled up," Dad said. "Keep your cool and stay in control."

"Rule five: Know your rights, or at least know what you're being stopped for," Troy said.

"Finally, rule six. And this wasn't written down, but something Grandpa Joe looked me in the eye and said." Dad cleared his throat. "'Son, think of your mama. What would she want you to do? What would she want to hear you did? Then get home and tell her yourself.'"

Dad fell silent, and the sound of his knife chopping up the bananas filled the kitchen. Mom wiped something from her eye. Troy and Ant wore grim looks. Chris and I looked at each other, and then I reached over and squeezed Mom's hand. She smiled, sniffed, and squeezed back.

"I know you're a good boy," she said. "I know it. I know all of you are good boys, 'cause your father and I raised you, and we made sure of it. But not everyone wants to think you are. And I don't want to get a phone call—"

She broke off and a tear rolled down her cheek. Dad gave the banana another vicious chop, then placed the knife down and leaned on the counter with both hands. I looked between the two of them, unsure of what to say. Mom finally let a ragged sigh out and looked around the table.

"I don't want a call saying I lost a son."

I looked up. Mom was looking at me, biting her lip. She saw something in my face, and she burst into tears, shoulders shaking so hard that Dad turned to wrap his arms around her. My mom and dad saw things I never did. Our interaction with those police officers had really shaken them up.

"I don't want a call like that," she said again, sobbing.

I got up before I even realized it, and I was hugging her too, and then everybody joined in for an impromptu Fairmont family hug. We all held one another, not speaking, but still letting each and every member of the family know how much they meant.

Mom giggled through her sniffles.

"One of y'all needs to go shower."

Troy stepped back and sniffed. "Jeez, Dad, have you been wrestling Ethan's guinea pig?"

The rest of us chuckled. Dad shoved Troy away and pointed a finger at him.

"Keep it up, boy, and you can kiss your serving of Bananas Foster goodbye."

Troy staggered back, a hand over his heart. "You wouldn't?! Mom, you hear this?"

Mom shrugged, wiping her eyes on the back of her hospital scrubs. "Your father and I present a united front always, baby. And besides—" she grinned and let Dad feed her a slice of banana. "It's just more for me."

Everybody laughed. Ant snuck a slice while Dad boxed out Troy, and just for a moment the world outside seemed so very far away.

Later that night, I sat against the attic wall with Nugget in my lap. The greedy furball had squeaked angrily at me for five minutes straight when I showed up late to give him dinner. He took a break from munching on a leaf of lettuce to squeak at me, little bits of green flying out of his mouth.

"*Ew*, dude, don't talk with your mouth full," I said, holding the lettuce as he nibbled at it.

He squeaked, and I scratched the top of his head.

"I'm a horrible friend," I whispered to him.

Nugget stopped chewing and twitched his nose at me.

"It's true," I said, letting my head fall back against the wall. "All this time, I thought Kareem was a traitor. I didn't understand how he could just leave me, then hang out with RJ. But I never thought to just ask him."

Something brushed my chin, and I looked down to see Nugget crawling up my shirt. The furry goofball tucked himself into the side of my neck and squeaked once.

"Yeah, I should go talk to him tomorrow."

More squeaks.

"After giving you breakfast. I know."

I yawned and stood up. Nugget squeaked as I carried him over to his cage. I rolled my eyes at him and gave him the rest of the lettuce. He jumped and kicked his legs up, then settled down to eat.

"Greedy butt," I muttered. I emptied my pockets, placing Cheese's metal flower on my desk and the half-eaten pickle next to it. I didn't even know I had it, or I would have given it to Cheese—it smelled like old trash and ear wax.

"Even you wouldn't touch that." I smiled at Nugget, who ignored me. Then I touched something wet on the side of my pants.

"*Ew*, is that pickle juice? That *is* pickle juice! Oh, it smells horrible! Jeez, Juan Carlos!"

I threw the pants in the corner, holding my nose as I saw drops on the floor where the pickle had apparently been leaking all this time. They led back to the stairs and down. I groaned. I'd have to clean that tomorrow or else Dad would have a fit. He was already going to have some questions the next time laundry time came around. Maybe I could sneak the pants in with the twins' gym socks.

Another yawn interrupted my diabolical plan. I flopped onto the bed, exhausted. Best friends, tiny aliens, and huge spaceships spun in my thoughts as I drifted off to sleep.

My eyes felt like they'd only just closed when something woke me up. The room was dark, and the only light came from the attic window Dad had installed to give me some fresh air. You opened it by turning a small crank, but I hardly ever did because it squeaked almost as loud as Nugget.

My eyes closed, then popped open again.

Something rustled in the dark a few feet away. Plastic crinkled, and a high-pitched sound came from out of the darkness.

"Nugget, if you climbed out of that cage to eat that pickle, I'm banning lettuce for a week. And no apples, either."

The plastic crinkled again.

"Super-Inventor-Geniuses need their sleep, furball! Otherwise we get cranky."

A squeak sounded from across the room. It came from Nugget's cage. I rolled over and grabbed the book-light I kept near my bed. The beam lit up the wall, then traveled down to Nugget's cage. I didn't see him at first, until something shifted in the corner. I spotted him hiding in his house.

"You okay, buddy?"

Nugget didn't answer. The guinea pig peeked out, then hid again.

Plastic crinkled again. I slowly swung the light across the room toward my desk—and nearly screamed as a bright, shiny silver creature loomed over me, six dark eyes staring at me, the remains of the hot-pickle wrapper disappearing into a wide mouth.

"Gurrfurr?"

14

A HOUSEGUEST!

Cheese stared at me from the attic darkness.

I stared back, confused.

Nugget stared at us both, sneaking bites of leftover lettuce while he watched.

"Cheese, what the fuzzlebutt are you doing here?" I whispered angrily.

The little shiny alien bobbed up and down. "Gtzey-gur—"

"Don't you try to explain this away, you metal meathead! Are you trying to get us both in trouble?"

I realized then that Cheese must've hidden in my book bag. No wonder we didn't see him when we left the factory. I crept out of bed and drew the hanging curtains around my area closed, making sure to press them tight against the wall. They hung from the floor to the ceiling, and I'd designed the setup for nights when for some reason I didn't want my parents to know I was still awake.

Hiding an alien seemed like a good reason.

"Do you know that there are people looking for you?" I asked, crawling back on top of my bed to sit cross-legged. "They're searching the whole neighborhood."

Cheese bobbed. Not being able to understand each other made things super-difficult.

Nugget peeked out from his cage and chirped.

The alien whirled high in the air, then zoomed over to the cage and stared at Nugget. The fuzzy little guinea pig chirped in alarm and dashed back into his hiding hole. Cheese looked at me.

"Gurrfurr?"

"No!" I shouted, then clapped my hands over my mouth. I lowered my voice. I started to see that "*gurrfurr*" had something to do with food. "Nugget is not food! He's a Nugget. Not a chicken nugget, but a guinea pig Nugget, and you don't eat those."

Cheese opened his mouth, and I saw the silver arm start to creep out.

"Guuuuuuurrfurr?"

I rolled off the bed and ran around to the cage, getting in between the hungry alien and Nugget, who trembled in the corner. Scooping him into my hands, I cradled my pet and scooted away from Cheese.

"Nugget. Isn't. Food! Look, stay here, I'll go get you something to eat. Stay!"

Cheese looked disappointed, and I pointed to a corner. "Stay there. I'll be right back with some snacks. Stay!"

The shiny alien dropped to a low hover above the floor and stared after me, its big eyes sad and wide. All six. I started to put Nugget back in the cage, but after thinking about it I decided to take him with me to the kitchen. Chunky little dude might end up as a snack if I left him.

Sneaking down to the kitchen is a tricky thing to do when an angry guinea pig is chirping in your ear. Nugget was going to get us caught.

"Hush," I whispered. "So, you almost got eaten. Big deal. Next time don't look so delicious."

Nugget chirped louder.

"Okay, okay, okay. I'm sorry, I'll make sure to remind Cheese not to eat you when we get back upstairs."

More chirping.

"Okay, 'ever.' I'll tell Cheese not to eat you ever."

Nugget nuzzled between my neck and cheek, still chirping angrily under his breath. I scratched his ears as I slipped open the door at the bottom of the attic stairs. Troy snored loudly on the couch, a line of drool hanging from the corner of his mouth. I made a face as I tiptoed past him. Ant and Chris shared a room near the back of the house. I crept past the cracked door.

The soft glow of the light above the stove lit the kitchen. I thanked whoever had left it on. Now I didn't have to risk turning on the bright overhead kitchen light. I rummaged through the cupboards with one hand, trying to find something a metal alien would enjoy.

"Do you think it'd like cereal?" I asked Nugget. "Something crunchy and sweet? No milk, though, that's just messy. Oh, what about rice? Everybody likes rice. Right? No? *Hmm.*"

I moved to the fridge and opened it.

"Jackpot!" I whispered.

Eight huge trays lined the inside of the fridge. All the other groceries and bottles had been squished to one side. I peeled back the aluminum foil on one tray. Dad's test batches of marinated chicken, some grilled and some baked, lay inside. I stuffed a sleepy Nugget into my front shirt pocket, ignoring his annoyed chirp, and got a paper plate and started loading up.

"They won't miss one or two pieces," I mumbled. After thinking about it, I grabbed two more, and a bottle of hot sauce. "Might as well have a snack myself."

Nugget chirped.

"Oh, cut it out, no one's eating your fuzzy butt. Now go to sleep."

I grabbed the cereal, the plate of chicken, and the hot sauce and hightailed it back to my room.

"You're in luck buddy, I found . . ."

My voice trailed off.

Cheese floated next to my desk, the metal flower I'd swiped from his ship floating in front of him. The petals were opened, and the hologram image made of golden dust played above them. Cheese and his family. In the darkness of my room, it was like watching a home movie come to light.

The alien turned to look at me and chirped sadly. I swallowed.

"I'm sorry. I know I shouldn't have taken it. I just . . . I wanted to know more about you. About why you're here, and what you're looking for."

Cheese turned back to the flower and touched it. The silvery petals folded back shut, and it floated back to land gently on my desk. The alien chirped something again. It sounded short, like one word.

"Is that your family?" I asked quietly.

Cheese didn't answer.

I thought about it, then snapped my fingers. I set the food down on the floor, placed a sleepy Nugget back in his cage, and moved to my desk. I rummaged through the top drawer, then pulled open the middle drawer and dug around inside.

"I know I saw it here the other day. What did I do with—aha!"

I stood and held up a dusty, black leather photo album. Mom had made it when I started middle school. She told me she had done it for me, but I think she liked to look at it just as much. Some of the pictures were super-old, some were just plain embarrassing. I flipped through to the back, looking for a specific one.

"Gotcha."

I pulled the photo out and tapped my finger in the middle as I held it out for Cheese to study.

"See this? This is my family." I couldn't see where my fingers landed, but I didn't have to—I knew every square inch of that photo.

It's the picture Kareem's parents took at my third-grade science fair. We were all standing in front of my winning project, a robotic pet on wheels that followed you and carried snacks. The judges had been impressed at how Barky 1.8 stopped when you stopped, followed you at your heels, and even lifted the platter on its back so you could reach the snacks.

Mom and Dad beamed with pride in the photo. Troy and Ant made funny faces, and Chris held bunny ears up behind my head. But there, front and center, I stood holding up my medal, and Kareem stood next to me, arm around my shoulders, smiling just as hard as I was.

"Family," I said again, softly.

Cheese leaned in close, then turned and lifted the metal flower off my desk. It hovered in midair and opened again when the alien touched it. We both watched the images play, the golden light sending flickering shadows across the bed; and when it was over, Cheese sank a little lower to the ground.

It chirped.

I held my picture up and pointed at it, then pointed at the flower. "Family."

Cheese chirped again, and I could sort of make out the sounds, though it didn't make sense. I mean, it was alien to me. Literally.

"Family," I said again.

"Skzgorp," Cheese said.

"Skzgorp?" I repeated, raising my eyebrows. "Family is skzgorp?"

Cheese spun in agreement.

Cheese brought its one arm out from underneath its mouth and tried to imitate the fist pump, but it looked more like a wet noodle. I shook my head and laughed.

"Okay, we'll work on that."

The alien tapped the photo I still held. "Skzgorp?"

I nodded. Cheese bobbed once or twice, then hovered closer and tapped in the middle of the photo where Kareem and I stood.

"Fa-moo-skzgorp?"

I nodded, a lump in my throat. "Yeah. He's family-skzgorp too."

Cheese bobbed again. It pointed at me, then pointed around my room. Then it pointed at itself, then tapped the picture of its spaceship in my sketchbook.

"Chzlwzkrpinpop lzrt."

I stared at the Pinball, then at Cheese, then back at the Pinball.

"Holy moly," I said. "That's your room? The Pinball is your room?"

The alien had an entire spaceship as its room! That was incredible! All that space!

I fell backward and put my hands behind my head, thinking about what I'd do if I had all that room. Nobody keeping their spare things next to your bed. No one dropping dirty clothes in the washing machine and neglecting to close the lid, so the smell of dirty socks filled the air. Nobody forgetting you were sleeping behind the curtains as they started to hammer away at a metal folding chair.

"So much space," I said. "Cheese, that has to be awesome. Why—"

I stopped talking when I realized that my alien buddy wasn't floating nearby. It'd gone back to the desk and was watching the metal flower's projection. I swallowed, realizing the problem.

Cheese had lost its family. Cheese had crashed here on Earth.

I looked down at the picture of me and my family, and Kareem, and the lump returned to my throat.

If I lost them, I'd want to try and find them too.

I stared at Kareem.

I couldn't imagine what it must feel like to have your family split apart . . . forever.

Family was everything.

"Cheese," I said, clenching my fists. "We'll help you. We'll get your ship fixed and you'll be flying back to your family in no time."

Cheese twirled to face me. "Fa-moo-lzrt?"

I nodded. "Family."

The little alien shivered, then shot up into the air and bobbed happily. It twirled three times. Super-Inventor-Genius Ethan Fairmont, future mayor of Ferrous City, had work to do. But first some rest was mandatory. I fell asleep to the sound of Cheese chomping the chicken, slurping the hot sauce like an Earthly delicacy.

15

A GRAND PLAN!

Somebody pounded on the attic door and jolted me out of my sleep.

"Ethan! Time to get up now! Ethan!"

I sat up, confused. A string of drool dangled from my mouth. Sunshine leaked through my wall of curtains. I rubbed my eyes and stared at the mess all around me. Colored pencils, loose paper with random scribbles, and a half-chewed shoe lay scattered on the covers. I blinked.

"Ethan? I swear, if you make me come up there. . . ." Dad's voice sounded muffled through the door at the bottom of the stairs. I started to answer, but I looked back at the shoe with a giant bite taken out of it.

"That does not look tasty," I said to myself.

The door to the attic opened and Dad's heavy footsteps shook the house.

"Boy, you'd better be unconscious or searching for your voice, 'cause I know you heard me calling you."

Something rustled in the corner, jostling the curtains next to Nugget's cage. A shiny head peeked over the edge of my bed. I'd forgotten about the alien!

Cheese chirped.

Oh crap.

I jumped out of bed. "Sorry, Dad. I heard you, I'm throwing on some clothes."

The footsteps paused, then kept coming.

"Is that my old hard hat?" Dad asked. "What did you do to it? I told you about using our things without asking, Ethan. Your mother told me what you did with her vacuum. I know you like inventing things, but you've got to show some respect for other people's stuff."

I pulled on some pants and stepped around the curtains just as Dad reached the top of the stairs. He raised an eyebrow at the separated room. I tugged the curtains closed and cleared my throat. Dad held up Nugget's Piggy Pack.

"Well? What is this?"

"Uh . . . it's a Piggy Pack."

"A what?"

"A Piggy Pack." I held out my hand, and after a second Dad handed it over. I strapped it on, then slipped behind the curtains, picked up a drowsy Nugget, tossed a dirty pair of sweatpants over a curious Cheese, then stepped back out. Dad's jaw dropped when I sat Nugget in the Piggy Pack and strapped him in.

"See?" I asked.

"Yes, I do see. You called it a piggy hat?"

"Piggy Pack."

"Right. Well, just make sure you ask before you use other people's stuff in your inventions, all right?"

Nugget chirped in alarm as he swung back and forth on top of my head. Dad couldn't hold back his laughter anymore. He patted me on the back, making Nugget swing even more.

"Wash up and come on down. Breakfast is on the table," Dad said, wiping a tear from his eye. He turned and started downstairs, then looked back at me and chuckled again before leaving.

The attic door closed, and I let out a sigh of relief.

"That was too close," I said, pulling back the curtains to let everyone get some light.

Cheese hovered just off the floor, as the sweatpants fell off of him. The alien floated up to my head and checked on Nugget, who let out an annoyed chirp. The alien and my guinea pig held a high-pitched conversation.

I slid off the bed, stretched, then grabbed my toothbrush and headed downstairs. "I'll grab some hay for you, Nugget; and Cheese, I'll find you something. Just try not to eat anything that's . . ." I gazed around the room and frowned. "Just try not to eat anything, okay?"

I left the room and raced downstairs to quickly grab a bit to eat. Homemade biscuits, sausage, and gravy sat on the kitchen table. Nobody else seemed to be around, so I stuffed several extra biscuits into my bathrobe. I thought about taking Cheese some gravy, but I didn't know how.

Dad walked into the kitchen just as I was pouring gravy into an old sippy cup I found in the back of the cupboard.

"You know we have apple juice, right?" Dad asked.

"Oh, yeah, right," I said. "But I just, uh . . . I just really love gravy."

"And why are you using a sippy cup?"

"Uh, nostalgia?"

Dad waited there, frowning, so I took a sip.

"*Mmm.*" The warm, lumpy sauce tasted salty, but I managed to swallow some. "Delicious."

Dad shook his head. "What a kid." He moved to the sink and started washing his hands.

"Where is everybody?" I asked. I tightened the cap on the sippy cup and slipped it next to the biscuits in my robe. Dad looked out the window.

"Summertime fun," he said, then whistled a short tune. "There was some commotion at the end of the block, your Mom said, but I haven't heard anything since. Your brothers left for the park an hour ago. Going to join them?"

"No. I've got other plans."

Dad studied me. "You don't seem too happy about it."

"It's not that. I'm just stuck on a problem. I don't know what to do next."

"Oh, like a math problem?"

"No, like a helping a friend problem."

"Well, it's the thought that counts."

I scoffed. "Thanks, Dad."

"Any time, son. And Ethan, be careful out there."

Dad got up, gave me an affectionate bump with his shoulder, grabbed another biscuit, and walked out of the room whistling. I quickly poured more gravy in the cup, snagged two more biscuits, then zoomed back up to the attic.

"All right," I said, once everyone had finished eating. "Here's the plan. We're going to go back to the factory and dig through Cheese's ship. There's got to be some clue that we can use to help fix that thing. Now let's take inventory."

Cheese looked up from dipping his one arm into the cup of gravy, and Nugget was in the middle of stuffing half a biscuit into his cheek. I dusted crumbs off my lap, then reached down and grabbed my Ready-to-Go backpack.

I'd gotten the idea for this by watching survival shows on television. Those people packed a bag full of supplies and kept it nearby so they'd always be prepared. But where they had rope and matches and a rain poncho in theirs, my bag was different.

I emptied the knapsack and sorted everything out.

"Two screwdrivers, a roll of duct tape, three smaller rolls of electrical tape—all different colors—one pair of needle-nose pliers, one pair of scissors, one pair of fuzzy socks. Wait a minute. Fuzzy socks? How did those get in here?"

I looked up at Cheese, who floated away with an innocent chirp. I rolled my eyes and finished checking off the items.

"One Swiss Army knife, a portable fan, three power packs, and one can of oven degreaser." I shook the can, then nodded. "Good, still half-full. This stuff is amazing. Well, that's it. Everyone ready?"

When I looked up from putting everything back in the knapsack, I saw the picture of me and Kareem and my family still lying out. I swallowed, knowing exactly what I needed to do. "We've got to bring family. We're gonna need their help too. Let's go get mine so you can go find yours."

Cheese bobbed and twirled with a happy chirp, Nugget jumped and kicked his legs up, and I laughed. I put Nugget in his cage with another half biscuit, helped Cheese climb inside the bag, then threw on some clothes. Time to go to work.

As soon as I stepped outside, I realized something was wrong. I couldn't say *exactly* what gave me the willies, but something didn't quite add up.

Big gray clouds hung in the sky, and if it hadn't been the middle of June I'd have thought a snowstorm was on the way. They hovered over Ferrous City, fat and scary. I shivered, even though it was hot outside.

But that didn't explain the tingly feeling I got. As I looked up and down the block, I realized what did.

"Where is everybody?" I asked under my breath.

The streets were empty. Nobody walked along the sidewalk. No cars drove up and down the block, no radios blared, no kids laughed. It looked so empty and abandoned that for a moment I panicked and poked my head back inside the house.

"Dad?" I called. "Dad, you in there?"

"Boy, quit yelling like the house is on fire," he shouted back from somewhere in the living room, and I sighed in relief. "What is it?"

"*Uh*, nothing, just . . . nothing, never mind."

"Well, shut the door! You're letting all the cool air out; and last time I checked, you didn't pay any electric bills!"

I closed the door, turned around, and took a deep breath.

"Okay, first thing first, get the gang together."

I could feel Cheese shifting in my backpack, twirling in agreement. Tightening my grip on the straps, I set off down the street to Juan Carlos's house. As I walked, the hairs on the back of my neck prickled, like someone was watching me. I glanced over my shoulder to see if I was being followed, but no, the streets remained empty.

Still, the feeling didn't leave. It seemed like at any moment something would leap from behind a bush or from inside a fence and grab me. I started walking faster. Something clattered against the side of a house as I sped past. I jumped fifty feet in the air.

Well, maybe not fifty, but I jumped.

"*Meow?*"

A cat hopped on the fence and started licking its paws. *Phew.* I jogged the last few feet to where Juan Carlos lived and knocked on the door. Nobody answered. I knocked again, harder, and was about to use both fists when the door opened a crack and a little old lady peeked out.

"Who are you?"

I cleared my throat. "Morning, ma'am. Is Juan Carlos home?"

"Who are you?"

"Oh, sorry, my name is Ethan Fairmont. I live down the street. Can Juan Carlos come outside?"

She poked her head out farther, and I could see white hair pulled up into a bun, with reading glasses pushed up over her forehead and another pair of glasses perched on the end of her nose. This had to be Juan Carlos's grandmother.

She looked me up and down, then looked outside and scanned the block. She frowned. "Juanito is on punishment right now. He can't come play today."

"Oh, he is?" I said, my hopes sinking. So much for getting the gang together.

"Yes, he was irresponsible; showing up home after curfew is unacceptable. Unacceptable!"

"Sorry," I said, intervening. I had to think quickly. "That's my fault. Juan was being a good friend. I lost my watch in the field and we spent all night looking for it. Juan was actually the one who found it. I hope he isn't in too much trouble, and

I'm sorry, Ms. Hernandez. It's too bad; we were just becoming really good friends."

I stopped to take a breath, and she stared at me suspiciously. A little tiny lie never hurt anybody. Especially when it's to get your friends out of the house to save an alien.

"*Hm*," she said, frowning. "Well, thank you for telling me, I guess. I didn't know."

"So, can Juan Carlos come out and play? Please? I'll be sure not to lose anything this time," I said hopefully.

Ms. Hernandez pushed up the glasses on her nose and squinted at me. I started to sweat. Some grandparents have the ability to read your every thought. My Grandma Ruby was like that, and it looked like Ms. Hernandez had that same power.

"Just a second," she said finally. She stepped back inside and closed the door. I fidgeted on the porch. I heard a muffled conversation and dared to hope. My mind started to drift to the light-flower and the mini-movie it played. Crap, the light-flower! In all the excitement, I had left it in my room.

After several seconds, the door opened all the way and Juan Carlos came out. He wore jogging pants and a sweatshirt with faded letters written across the chest.

"Hi, Ethan," he said, embarrassed.

"'Sup, man?" I punched him softly on the shoulder, then stood up straight as Ms. Hernandez moved onto the porch with us.

"Remember what I said, Juanito," she warned him with a wagging finger; then she said something in Spanish.

He nodded. "Sí, Abuela."

"Stay out of trouble," she warned us.

"Yes, ma'am, and thank you, ma'am," I said with the biggest smile I could manage.

She looked at me and squinted.

I kept smiling.

She squinted some more.

My cheeks were starting to hurt, but I kept that smile as wide as I could.

She snorted. "Get out of here, you two." She stepped back inside, and just for a second I saw a tiny smile cross her face before the door closed.

"*Whew*," I said, rubbing my jaw. "That was close."

Juan Carlos shifted, still embarrassed, and I punched him again.

"Hey, c'mon, man. It's not that bad. At least you can come outside, right?"

He stood there, uncomfortable. "She made me wear my cousin's old shoe, though. She said I wasn't ruining any more school shoes."

We looked down at his feet. On one foot he had the remaining shoe that Cheese hadn't eaten. On the other foot was a too-big blue sneaker.

"Oh. Well, it looks . . . fine? It's fine. C'mon, let's go get a snack from Jorge's before we find Kareem."

We walked down the block in silence for a few seconds. Juan Carlos kept looking at me, then looking down, then looking at me. Finally, he worked up the courage and cleared his throat.

"Thanks, Ethan. For talking to mi abuela."

"Hey, man, no problem. That's what friends are for, right?" I started to punch his shoulder again, but he dodged and snuck his own punch in.

"Yeah. That's what friends are for," he said, grinning.

I rubbed my arm and laughed, and he joined in. We walked together, talking about all the times we got in trouble, what we had to do to make it up to our parents. We talked about being kids who didn't always fit in and how that made us feel. I was beginning to see why talking to new people was so important. Juan Carlos was actually . . . great. We fell out laughing telling each other jokes, until Juan suddenly froze.

"What's wrong?" I asked.

He shushed me and pulled me behind a group of trash cans on the corner.

"Look," he said, pointing to the corner.

I took a peek, and my heart sank into my socks.

Police had a checkpoint up ahead, and a long line of cars started to form, a traffic backup like I've never seen. A few people honked, a few people shouted, a few people even stepped outside their cars for some air. I tugged at Juan Carlos.

"C'mon, Jorge's is on this side. We can watch from the windows inside his store."

We snuck up the street and slipped inside Jorge's Bodega. The store wasn't actually open yet, but Jorge himself stood just inside the door, arms folded, glaring at the fuss. He started to snap at us, then realized who we were.

"Boys, what are you doing out here? It's crazy right now," he said, pushing us inside.

"What's going on, Mr. Jorge?" I asked.

He scowled, then picked up a broom and started sweeping the same section of floor with short, tight strokes. "Nonsense, that's what. Cops put a checkpoint out there. A checkpoint! Not letting people pass without looking in their cars. They've got two dudes in suits searching people's trunks!"

Juan Carlos and I looked at each other, both thinking the same thing.

Cheese.

"Y'all should get your friend and get on outta here," Jorge continued.

I looked up, startled. "What friend?"

"Kareem. Isn't that him right there?" Jorge jerked his chin at the window. "On the other side of the street?"

Sheesh, I thought he meant Cheese. I wiped some of the early-morning humidity off the window. The sidewalks were crowded as people got out of their cars to see what the holdup was, joining pedestrians and other storefront owners like Jorge. I could hear the noise from inside. It was a hundred jumbled, muddled conversations all mixing together, none of them happy. I was so focused on trying to pick out what everyone was saying that I almost missed the bright orange, yellow, and black T-shirt that slipped around the edge of the crowd. There he was, sitting on his Huffy bike.

"That *is* Kareem," I said out loud.

I've only known one person who wore dashiki print T-shirts. Kareem's uncle had a store up near Chicago, and he sent down shirts for everyone in the family. I had one myself, a present from the family for my birthday a few years back.

Kareem skulked back in the crowd, looking for a good way to cross to our side of the street. I waved at him, trying to get his attention, but there was too much going on.

Jorge glared at the cops. "You can't just do this to people. It's not right."

We watched as a woman and her kids were escorted out of an old station wagon, and the cops searched the trunk.

"Wouldn't happen in a white community, I'll tell you that much," Jorge muttered.

My heartbeat could probably be seen through my shirt. I was nervous. Really nervous. My palms were sweating like a leaky faucet. I would have been nervous enough on my own—especially after The Talk last night—but the stakes were even higher, thanks to Cheese. I could feel the alien's extra weight in my backpack, and it suddenly felt as heavy as an elephant. If Cheese would have just stayed with the Pinball. . . .

"We've got to get back to the factory," I whispered to Juan Carlos. "Like, *now*."

"I don't think anybody's gonna be doing much 'hanging out,'" Jorge muttered. He shook his head. "Looks like they're turning everybody away from our block, boys. Don't make sense."

Turning people away from our block.

They didn't want anyone coming in. Or going out.

"It's not right," Jorge said suddenly. "Just when this city was on the rebound from the factory shutting down, they wanna pull this?"

Jorge gripped his broom. "Hang on, boys. This isn't happening in my community, not while Jorge Ruiz still pays his taxes!"

Jorge stomped out of the store.

"Taxes?" Juan Carlos asked after a moment.

I shrugged. "Adults give money away like they don't want it."

Jorge stepped off the curb and walked into the middle of the intersection, shouting at the police while flailing his broom. A few people pointed and nudged their neighbors. Soon everybody was watching as the cops approached Jorge to calm him down.

One walked up. "Sir, I need you to step back on the side-walk, please."

"And I need you to have a real reason to search these people's cars!" Jorge snapped back. "You can't do this! Tell us what's going on!"

While Jorge went back and forth with the officers, I snuck out of the shop and whistled. Kareem's eyes zipped over to me. I motioned him over. He shifted his gaze to the cops, but they were busy with Jorge. I gestured for Kareem to hurry, and after one more tentative look, he rode his bike across the street.

"Hey," I said.

"Hey," Kareem responded, jumping off his bike.

Kareem and I had left things on a bit of an awkward note. I still felt bad about not being there for him when he needed me.

"Kareem, I wanted to say . . . I'm sorry, man. I had no idea. I just don't know why you didn't tell me."

"It's not something you brag about, you know? You have the perfect family, and I was just . . . embarrassed."

I had no idea Kareem felt that way. I know I hold it together well, but our family was far from perfect.

"Kareem, you're my best friend. You don't ever have to be embarrassed to tell me anything."

Kareem studied his feet. "Thanks bro, that means a lot to me. I was actually headed to your block to apologize to y'all. Sorry for snapping like that, I shouldn't have."

Kareem stuck his hand out. I dapped him up and pulled him in for a hug. I think he might've shed a tear.

Kareem quickly changed the subject. "But anyway, how's Cheese?"

"Well, if we don't fix Cheese's ship, sooner or later those cops are gonna find him with the Others."

"The Others?"

I gave a quick summary of the two people in suits searching the neighborhood—first outside the barbershop, and then outside my house last night.

"You know, now that I think about it, I've seen them too," he said.

"The Others," Juan Carlos whispered, then shuddered. "What were they looking for?"

"They said a 'fugitive,' but I'm positive they mean Cheese," I said. I felt the little alien wiggle in my backpack, and I prayed it wouldn't choose now to pop out.

Juan Carlos looked extra-nervous and started glancing back over his shoulder. "How can we fix the ship? You got any ideas?"

"Not yet. But I know how to get some, and I'm gonna need your help. Both of you."

Kareem stayed quiet for a second, then shrugged. At least I think it was a shrug. He might've been gasping for air. It was hard to tell. Juan Carlos had a terrified look on his face, but he clenched his fists and nodded.

"I'll help," he said.

"I'm definitely in," Kareem said. "For Cheese."

"Thanks," I said. I knew we weren't back where we'd been once, but it was a start.

We rushed across the field full of weeds and bushes and stopped at the end of the block. The factory loomed over the treetops like a sleeping giant. All three of us gripped the cold metal fence. Time was running out. We had to fix Cheese's ship before the cops and the weird people in suits came looking for us.

I swallowed. "All right, boys. Now or never."

With that, we all ducked under the hole in the fence. No time for Magna-gloves today.

LET'S HOPE THAT'S REALLY POLLEN

Nobody spoke as we approached the factory. The cops on the corner, the conversation with my parents and brothers last night, Cheese. Things didn't make sense right now. It was like putting a puzzle together without using the picture on the box as a guide.

The clouds overhead had gotten even heavier. They hung right over the factory, as if waiting for us to step inside before the storm started. We hurried across the field, hopping over broken bottles and sidestepping ditches filled with dirty water.

"The news said it wasn't supposed to rain today," Juan Carlos muttered.

"You watch the news?" Kareem asked.

"Mi abuela does. She likes to know what's happening, I guess. Anyway, the weather report said it was supposed to be sunny today."

"Weather people are always getting stuff wrong."

"I know, right? This one time . . ."

They started talking about the different times the weather forecast had been totally off, but I stopped listening. Cheese had started wriggling around in my backpack. We were nearly at the factory door and there was no one in sight. Just an empty field of weeds and grass that stretched back to the fence.

"Okay, fine," I said, then knelt down and unzipped my backpack. Cheese popped out with a twirling chirp. "'Sup, buddy?" I said.

Cheese whizzed around me, its little blue hover-cloud sparkling under the gray skies. Cheese zoomed over to Juan Carlos and Kareem, interrupting their conversation.

I pulled a biscuit out of my pocket and tossed it to him. "Here, I know you're probably hungry."

The silver arm shot out from beneath its mouth and snagged the biscuit in midair. While Cheese ate, I turned to Juan Carlos and Kareem. They both still looked amazed.

"You took Cheese home?" Juan Carlos asked.

"It was more of a stowaway situation, but it worked out," I said. I stepped up to the secret entrance and gestured for the two boys and the small alien covered in biscuit crumbs to follow. "Come on, I'll tell you what happened to it, and how we're going to help."

Inside, we quickly made our way to the back of the factory. Right away, I could tell something was different. I wasn't the only one.

"Ethan, did you come back here without us last night?" Juan Carlos asked, gazing around.

I could see why he thought that—the whole area was re-arranged. Factory stuff moved, footprints in the dust everywhere, even in areas I knew for sure we hadn't walked. Some of the old plastic tarps that usually cloaked some equipment had been thrown off, lying on the floor like dirty clothes.

"No way," I said. "But somebody else did."

"Look," said Kareem, pointing. Cheese whirled over to where he stood, pointing down at the muddy ground. Juan Carlos and I followed. "Check out these footprints. Those aren't sneaker treads!"

He was right. The sneaker prints we'd just left when we walked in were obvious. You could even see the swoosh logo on Kareem's. But the ones we stood over, dried in mud, were different.

"Those are hard shoes," Kareem said confidently. "Church shoes or something."

"Or cop shoes," I said quietly.

"Oh man," Juan Carlos said. "Do you think they found . . . ?"

"Oh no!" I cried. I hadn't even thought of that. All of us turned and raced over to the brick wall and its nook where we'd hidden the Pinball.

Oh, please don't let them have found it.

"Thank *goodness*," Kareem nearly shouted.

There it was. Cheese's ship was where we'd stowed it, hidden behind the screen of the old factory equipment. I sighed with relief. What if the cops or the Others had found it and taken it away? Clearly they had been here, searching the Factory. It was pure luck that they hadn't found the Pinball—or Cheese. I was suddenly super-glad that the little alien had hidden in my backpack and come home with me.

"Okay, so what next?" Juan Carlos said.

I pulled out my sketchbook, stepped back out into the sunlight that poured in through the hole in the ceiling, and cleared a spot on the floor. We all huddled around.

"All right," I said. "Here's the story."

I quickly told Kareem and Juan Carlos about Cheese and its family and what I'd seen inside its ship.

Kareem shook his head. "But how? How did Cheese get separated? What made the ship crash?"

Cheese started to bob in distress. I patted its small shiny back.

"I don't know. All I can tell is it makes Cheese very upset. And very afraid."

Juan Carlos gulped. "So what's the plan?"

"I'm glad you asked. Juan Carlos, I need you to work with Cheese some more. See if you can figure out anything else about what happened."

Juan Carlos nodded.

"If you need something, whistle, and we'll come on out."

I turned to Kareem. "We're going back inside the Pinball."

"Wait, what?" Kareem's eyebrows shot up to the top of his forehead. "Inside? Are you sure that's safe?"

I nodded. "I've been in once and I'm fine. I think it's a chance we can take. We need to understand this ship if we're going to fix it for Cheese."

Kareem took a deep breath. "Okay, fine."

"Come on," I said. "Just like before. Super-inventor squad, remember?"

I held out my fist. Kareem stared at it, then made a fist of his own and we banged them together.

"I never forgot," he said. "Super-inventor squad."

We walked up to the ship. Cheese chirped and the middle of the ship opened. Kareem and I climbed inside. I didn't know if we were *best* friends again, but we were friends at least, and honestly? That made things seem not quite as strange.

"Cheese and crackers," Kareem whispered. He was just as impressed as I was.

We stood just inside the Pinball. I nudged a metal flower aside with my foot. The petals curled back and a tiny sprinkle of golden dust fell out.

"Is that pollen?" Kareem asked.

"Seems that way," I said. It made sense. Earth flowers had pollen, so maybe alien flowers had it too. It's just that their pollen floated in the air and played alien movies.

"Okay, so where should we start? It's pretty empty."

I headed over to the control panel. Some of the controls that had been dim last time had completely faded.

"It's running out of power," I said to myself.

"What?" Kareem called.

"The ship. It's running out of power. You know when you have a toy that's getting old, and the batteries start to run out?"

"Yeah, like that superhero doll you used to play with all the time."

"It was an *action figure*, not a doll," I said. "Anyway, I think the ship is running out of power, and that's the problem. I bet it burned its last energy when it expanded."

"Expanded?"

"Well, when Juan and I made first contact, the ship was much smaller, maybe the size of a small boulder. But it grew, I think to try to scare us off."

"So the metal can stretch, like rubber?" Kareem asked.

A thought hit me.

"Kareem, you're a genius. Rubber. Rubber comes from plants. Look around, these flowers might produce metal and rubber. Or Metal-Rubber. Or Rubber-Metal? Anyway, if so, this tech could change everything on Earth. Amazing."

I walked around the room, looking for more clues about the ship. I picked up broken metal flowers and moved aside piles of the pollen that came from them. I didn't see anything else in the ship that gave me clues.

What am I missing?

Just then, a sharp whistle echoed through the room.

"That came from outside the ship," Kareem said.

"It's Juan Carlos," I said, running to the entrance. "He needs our help!"

17

SHOULD YOU RESCUE YOUR OWN BULLY?

We leaped out of the Pinball.

"What is it?" I shouted at Juan Carlos.

"*Shh*," he said, waving his hands. "Come take a look at this."

He and Cheese were huddled on top of a stack of crates next to the back wall. They were sneaking looks out of a long rectangular window high up near the ceiling.

"How did y'all get up there?"

"*Shhhh!* Just come here."

Kareem and I scrambled up the dusty wooden crates and crouched down below the window ledge. Cobwebs tickled my neck and head. I flailed wildly, almost slapping myself in the face. Cheese twirled and flashed us a limp fist pump. Kareem stared at the alien in confusion.

"I'll explain later," I said.

"Look," Juan Carlos said, pointing out the window.

"What is it?"

"Just look!"

It took me a few seconds to figure out what Cheese and Juan Carlos were looking at, but when I saw, my eyes narrowed. The last person I expected to see stood below us outside the factory.

"RJ?" Kareem said. "What's RJ doing here?"

"It's not just him," Juan Carlos whispered.

The dude who'd made my life miserable for the last two years stood yelling at somebody hidden behind the corner of the factory. Di stood behind him with her arms crossed. I couldn't see who they were angry at, but I could hear RJ's muffled voice as he complained about something.

They stood in the cracked and weed-filled parking lot. RJ and Di both faced the factory. If they looked up, they'd see us all peeking out the window. But something, or someone, held their attention.

"I don't get it," I said. "Why are they here? And who are they yelling at?"

Kareem shrugged but didn't say anything. Juan Carlos thought about it for a second.

"I guess they're looking for us, maybe?"

"Why can't they just leave us alone?" I muttered.

We continued to watch, but whoever they were yelling at didn't seem to care. RJ threw up his hands and spun around. To our surprise, he got on his knees and put his hands on top of his head. Di looked unhappy, maybe even scared, but she did the same.

"What are they doing?" Juan Carlos asked.

Kareem was silent while I started to fiddle with the locks on the window. "I don't know, but I can't hear. I don't like them, and whoever else is down there, so close to Cheese's ship."

Cheese bobbed in agreement.

"Right." I finally worked the locks free and pushed the window outward. "I don't want anyone to find—"

"*Shhh!*" Juan Carlos interrupted and dragged me down from the window.

The rusty hinges on the window creaked as it swung outward. I glared at Juan Carlos, but he held a finger up over his lips. His eyes were wide. He mouthed a word, but I didn't understand. I looked back over the window ledge and froze.

Two cops were standing in the parking lot.

One stood behind RJ and had his handcuffs out.

The other was looking up at the window where we were peeking out.

I almost yelped, but thankfully nothing came out. That's how scared I was. The cop held her hands over her eyes to help her see better, but after a moment she turned back to stand over Di.

"Why are the cops here?" Kareem whispered.

"I don't know," Juan Carlos whispered back.

"Hold on," I said, straining to hear what the cops were telling RJ and Di. "*Shhh.*"

The first cop, a tall man with a mustache, pointed at the two kids and shook his handcuffs at them.

"If you kids didn't do anything, why did you start running?" he was asking.

Even though RJ was kneeling and facing the other way, I could hear his shouts from up here.

"'Cuz y'all just rolled up on us like somebody was shooting," RJ yelled back.

"Well, if you would have just sat there and answered our questions, we could have—"

"Answer your questions? Man, I saw how y'all treated Rick the Barber when *he* answered your questions."

I glanced at Kareem and Juan Carlos in surprise. *RJ had been there too? Had he been following us this whole time? What had he seen? Did he know about Cheese?* The questions flew around my head, and I almost missed the conversation below.

"That was different," said the other cop, a lady with dark hair pulled back into a ponytail.

"Different how?" RJ asked. "He didn't do anything either, and y'all grabbed him and started hitting him with this metal stick."

"We didn't *hit* him," Mustache Cop said. "It's a—well, never mind what it is, but it helps us figure out if you're telling the truth."

RJ snorted. "Yeah, by beating it out of people."

"Now look, that's enough! You're coming back with us and you're going to answer some questions, and then we'll take you back to your parents."

"Man, we didn't do anything!"

"We can start with trespassing on this property."

"You chased us here!"

The cops stepped up behind RJ and Di and put the hand-cuffs on them. RJ shouted and yelled back at the cops, but Di stood quiet with a frightened look on her face.

I didn't like them. I especially didn't like RJ. Actually, that's not quite true.

I really, really, really, really, really didn't like RJ.

But as we watched the two cops hustle them away and out of sight, a sick feeling bubbled in the pit of my stomach. They hadn't done anything wrong. Those cops and the Others were looking for Cheese. The longer our alien friend stayed here, the more danger it was in, and that also meant more harassment our peaceful neighborhood would have to suffer through.

Even RJ didn't deserve that.

CHEESE TELLS A STORY

I heard a rattling sound, and I looked over to see Cheese shaking as it peered out the window too. It had a sad expression on its face. Something seemed wrong, and I leaned forward.

"What's up, Cheese?

The alien bobbed in distress.

"What is it?" I asked.

Cheese twirled and floated down the stack of crates, waiting for us.

"Okay, I guess we're following Cheese," I said.

We all scrambled down to the floor, then watched as Cheese took off for the Pinball.

"Cheese, hold up, where are you going?" I called.

Cheese zipped into the ship.

"Oh man, we have to go inside," Juan Carlos whispered. I patted him on his back.

"Don't worry, it's actually pretty cool in there."

Juan Carlos gulped.

"If you say so."

When we got inside the control room, and after a lot of *oohing* and *aahing* from Juan Carlos, we found Cheese by the giant golden metal flower growing out of the floor in the corner.

"Oh hey, we were going to ask you about that," I said to Cheese as we walked up to it.

Cheese had its back to us and I couldn't tell what it was doing. Glimmers of light flashed and little puffs of the golden pollen twinkled up into the air.

Juan Carlos's eyes grew wide. "This is the coolest thing I've ever seen in my life," he whispered.

Kareem smiled. "Yeah, it is, isn't it?"

Cheese turned around. The alien's silver arm waved around the room. We all grew quiet.

"Chzlwzkrpinpop lzrt." It looked at Juan Carlos, who made "go on" gestures, and the alien bobbed nervously.

Cheese twirled and picked up a light flower, its six eyes growing sad as it stroked the flower and petals crumbled to the floor.

The alien floated around to the side of the giant light-flower growing out of the floor. It touched one of the petals and the flower opened.

Golden pollen drifted out in curling lines, like glowing floating rivers. They curled up to the ceiling and stretched out around the room. When the pollen touched the controls for the Pinball, they lit up as if they were working again. When it touched the giant display on the wall, the display flickered to life before fading away.

But when one stream of pollen touched another, they combined to form shapes that seemed to move in the twinkling light. We sat in awe and watched the beautiful show, until I slapped my forehead.

"It's a giant-flower movie," I said. Kareem and Juan Carlos looked at me strangely. I tried to explain. "I saw these earlier, except the light-flowers were much smaller, and they played little movies. I accidentally left one back in my room."

"So, what does it do?" Kareem asked.

"Watch," I said. "I think we're going to see something amazing."

As the light expanded, pictures came to life. Cheese and his family were pulling light-flowers up from the ground.

Cheese swirled its arm again really fast, up and down and around and around. I got dizzy trying to watch it. Finally, the swirling stopped and we all sat forward in our seats.

"*Whooaaaaa*," we said at once.

More aliens just like Cheese flocked to him and his family in Pinballs. They collected light-flowers from Cheese's family and took them on their ships.

No Pinball was the same as another. Each ship slowly bobbed and twirled. Every so often, a sprinkle of light would tumble from the tops of the ships and fall to the planet's floor.

"What are they doing?" Juan Carlos whispered.

Something clicked in my head. "Wait, did you and your family make the light-flowers?"

Cheese stared at me. I motioned to the light-flower, then pretended to pass it to me, then to Kareem, then to Juan. Cheese spun with excitement. *Yes!* Cheese and his family shared these with others back on his planet. These light-flowers gave their ships energy.

Cheese twirled high in the air, scattering the golden pollen into a shower of glitter. "Cheese and crackers, cheese and crackers!"

But then Cheese slowly stopped twirling and sank to the floor.

"What's wrong?" I asked.

Cheese looked at us, then stirred up the pollen into another light-story. When Cheese finished, we gasped.

"What is that?" I asked, a shiver running down my spine.

"*Ahhh!*" Juan Carlos screamed, hiding his face in his arms.

Kareem clenched his fists so tightly, I thought his hands might turn purple.

A twisted snake creature—with one wing sticking out from its back and three sharp tails—appeared in the sky. It charged at Cheese and the other Pinballs. Then another creature appeared, and another, until each ship had a snake creature clinging on to it.

Juan Carlos peeked up over his arm at the light-story and shuddered. Cheese bobbed sadly just above the floor.

Kareem cleared his throat and pointed at the light-thieves. "What do those things want?"

"They want light-flowers," I replied before I could even think. "If these light-flowers are that powerful, maybe these creatures want to take them. Like, light-thieves."

Cheese swirled a small section of pollen, and another movie played.

The ships raced from the planet's surface to the sky, trying to escape. Several of the snake creatures cornered the ships, ripping and clawing inside, grabbing at the light-flowers. Their three sharp tails stabbed at whatever was in reach like a fork, and they swallowed up every light-flower in sight. With every gulp, they grew bigger and bigger. Some even grew additional tails or wings as they scarfed down light-flowers. Some changed into other forms before going back to being snakelike.

"JEEZ!" Juan exclaimed.

"They can shape-shift," Kareem mumbled.

I didn't say a thing. I was frozen by the idea of those things having an endless supply of light-flowers—they'd probably wipe out Cheese's whole family! Maybe even his whole species.

"This is awful," I finally whispered.

Cheese swirled another movie up. We watched as Pinballs started to leave the planet and enter outer space, only to be trapped by more snake creatures. The light-thieves took over the Pinballs while the little aliens were herded to a giant dome-shaped spaceship. Hundreds upon hundreds of little aliens were stuffed inside the dome.

Cheese stopped floating altogether and sank to the floor. It swirled its arm sadly one last time. Another image swirled to life.

Several ships, connected by tentacles, jetted off into space as the snake creatures chased them like dragons.

One light-thief was faster than the others. It caught up to the ships and started biting and whipping its tail at them. The Pinballs shook and rattled, and finally one separated and fell away. Everyone ignored it as the rest of the Pinballs and the snake creatures zoomed away.

"Is that . . . ?" Juan Carlos started to ask.

"It is," Kareem said.

We watched as the lone ship fell through space toward a blue planet. It tumbled around and around. When it finally hit the planet, I closed my eyes.

"That's how you came to Earth," I said. "You got separated from your family, and now you can't find them."

Cheese floated off the floor and hovered next to me. Alien or human, I knew when somebody was feeling sad and missed their family. At least, now I knew. I wasn't going to make the same mistake that I had with Kareem.

I threw an arm around Cheese, gave it a small hug. "Well, you're here now, and that means you're one of us. Right, guys?"

Kareem and Juan Carlos jumped to their feet and came over. "That's right," Kareem said. "As long as you're here, we've got your back."

Cheese twirled around, confused.

"No, we didn't actually take your back," I said, smiling. "It means we're going to help you, 'cause that's what friends do."

Juan Carlos nodded and smiled. "Friends welcome you, even if you're new and alone and scared."

Kareem said, "Friends are there for you when you feel like everything is going wrong, and they take you back even if you made a mistake." Kareem and I bumped fists.

I cleared my throat. "And most importantly, friends help each other out when there's a problem."

OPERATION GET CHEESE HOME!

We stood outside the ship, staring at the damage.

"It seems the light-flowers power the ship," I said. "And I think I know where they go. Under the ship, there's an opening that looks like a reactor. I'm pretty sure that's where we put the fuel. In this case, the light-flowers."

"Ahh, where do we get light-flowers?" Kareem asked. "Most of the ones on the ship are destroyed."

"I think they grow on the ship, but only when the ship is working. It's quite the conundrum," I admitted.

"Then we'll never get this thing to work," Juan said.

If you weren't a super-genius science inventor, I could see how one would draw that conclusion. Luckily, I was just that.

"There has to be a backdoor."

"A what?"

"A backdoor. That's a design flaw otherwise. There has to be a way to get the flowers to grow, even if the ship is out of power. If we can figure out what the ship needs to grow light-flowers, I think we can use them to get the ship back up and running."

Cheese bobbed up and down. It seemed it liked what I had to say.

"We know the plants are made of some sort of metal-rubber. So maybe if we feed the ship those two things, it'll power up."

"There's metal and rubber all over this place." Juan Carlos said.

"The ship must need something specific, something that's not here," I said. "Or else Cheese would have found it already."

Kareem and I stared at each other, each of us thinking the same thing. If Cheese wasn't using the scraps in the factory, we had to find another source of supplies. . . .

"Gadget Beach!"

"You mean that place by the river?" Juan Carlos asked.

"Yeah," Kareem said excitedly. "There's tons of metal, rubber, plastic, whatever you need."

"Right," I said, just as excited. "We need to bring back whatever we can find."

Cheese twirled in place. "Cheese and crackers!"

It turned out that hauling spaceship food back up to the factory storeroom would be easier said than done. We propped open the door leading from the factory to the river running beneath it, firmly telling Cheese to stay with the Pinball. Still, it was a long walk along the riverbank to Gadget Beach.

We gathered all the spare metal and rubber around, which seemed to be much less than I remembered. It's always when you need something that you can never find it. I looked at the small heap of old gadgets, electronics, tires, and knick-knacks.

"This should just about do it. It's going to have to."

"I'm tired, Ethan, and this stuff is heavy," Juan complained.

I couldn't blame him. We were all exhausted and the pile of ship food had to weigh at least as much as all of us combined. Three sixth-graders would have a hard time dragging it back to the factory. We needed something to help us out.

Was I a super-genius-inventor, or not?

A few planks of wood were floating just on top of the water. I pulled them in and quickly wove them together with vines from the nearby bushes. Voilà! We had a raft.

"Uh . . . are you sure this is going to work, Ethan?" Juan Carlos asked.

"Sure! I think." I scratched my head. "Maybe. I don't really know."

Juan Carlos stood on the wooden raft I'd built on the river-bank. I grabbed my handheld fan from my bag and fastened it to the back to act as a motor. Juan Carlos had a scared look on his face.

"Don't worry about it," Kareem called. "It's just like a paddleboat."

Juan Carlos stared at him, then stared at me, then stared at the paddleboat and swallowed.

"Are you ready?" I asked.

Juan Carlos shook his head. "Nuh-uh."

"Dude, come on, we've got to do this."

"Well, why can't one of you do it?"

"We're too big for it," I explained. "Plus you need me on this side when something goes wrong."

"*When* something goes wrong?!" Juan Carlos shouted.

I winced. "I mean *if* something goes wrong. *If!* But it shouldn't!"

"Okay, all done," Kareem called out as he finished loading the raft with our findings.

"Perfect, let's—"

I started to say something, but a muffled yelp from Juan Carlos got my attention. He was flailing his arms and pointing down the riverbank.

"What is it?" I called down to him.

He pointed again, this time with both hands. I turned to look and froze.

The Others.

There they were, off in the distance. The two suits were walking around, waving what must have been some sort of alien detector. I'm not sure how they'd found us, but they were too close for comfort. Time was running out. One of the suits looked our way and shouted, "Hey! Hey!"

"RUN, KAREEM!" I shouted, pulling him toward the river and the paddleboat.

If they wanded us with that machine, they'd absolutely realize we'd been with Cheese.

We scrambled onto the raft with Juan Carlos. The boat started to sink. I reached for the fan and jammed on the GO button. The fan turned on and started spinning. The paddleboat jerked forward, then picked up speed. We raced off down the river, leaving the Others yelling after us.

LATE, LATE, LATE!

We walked slowly up a dirt trail from the riverbank to the factory, dragging the dying paddleboat behind us. We'd managed to hold on to most of what we found, though we'd had to ditch some of our heavier gear to keep from sinking. Kareem tried to wring his shirt out, Juan Carlos's shoes made squelching sounds with each footstep, and I hopped on one foot trying to get water out of my ear.

By the time we got back to the factory, we were exhausted and hungry. And by Cheese's reaction, it was at least the second one. But snack time had to wait. We needed to test the theory of whether the metal and rubber would fire up Cheese's ship. If it did, Cheese could be snacking with its family in a millisecond instead of eating hot sauce.

But when we showed Cheese the stuff we had found, it didn't spin around in excitement as I had hoped. Cheese looked confused.

"Cheese and crackers?" he said, and nibbled a tire.

"Well, no," I said. "We thought this could fix your ship. Yes? Maybe? You know?"

Cheese flew back and forth between us and the Pinball, like he was pacing.

"Man, the language barrier is tough," Kareem said, rubbing the back of his neck.

Juan Carlos nodded. I rubbed my temples in frustration.

With Cheese by my side, I tried to mime filling up a gas tank, but there's no way an alien spaceship used something as primitive as gas.

"I don't know why I thought this would work," I growled to myself. "Why would a bunch of junk work?"

"Wishful thinking." Kareem shrugged. "I hoped it would work, too, because then all that junk at Gadget Beach would have a real purpose."

"It has a purpose," I said irritably. "I use it to make stuff all the time. Junk is okay when you can recycle it."

"Maybe Cheese's species doesn't have junk," Juan Carlos said. He looked up at the sky through the hole the Pinball crash had left. "Maybe they figured out solar energy better than we have."

Just then, a flock of pigeons flew over the hole. We all watched as something dropped down from the sky and landed—splat—on Juan Carlos's shoe.

He stared at the tiny explosion of pigeon poop.

"I'm ready to go home." Juan Carlos shook his head. "This day—I just want to go home," he said again.

As much as I wanted to laugh, I could only groan. "Me too."

"Yeah, me three."

I sighed deeply. Cheese was inside his ship, fiddling around, and didn't answer when I called. I guess we all needed a break from disappointment.

"Let's go to the bodega," I said. "We'll get something for us *and* Cheese."

Still dripping wet, we headed to Jorge's. Throughout the neighborhood there was an eerie silence. Nobody on the porches, nobody watering their lawns. Just silence.

"Where is everybody?" Juan Carlos asked.

Something moved in the corner of my eye. I looked up at the second-floor window of an old brown brick house. A curtain shifted a bit, as whoever was watching us ducked out of sight.

"I think they're hiding."

"From what?" Kareem asked.

"The cops? Or maybe they just have the same bad feeling I have."

By the time we reached Jorge's Bodega, we were more than a little cranky.

Kareem stopped at the corner and peeked around.

"Anything?" I asked him. I had to use the bathroom. Apparently a lot of the river water had gone in me, as well as on me.

"What are you three doing?"

I groaned as a familiar voice came from inside Jorge's Bodega. My older brother Troy stood in the doorway, wearing his uniform. He held a broom in his hand and had a smug look on his face. I knew that look. I didn't like that look. It was the look of an older sibling who knew he'd caught his younger brother doing something he wasn't supposed to. Now the only question was how much it would cost me.

"Uh, hey, Troy," I said.

He looked at me, then at Juan Carlos and Kareem. His eyes rested on Kareem for a second before he turned back toward me.

"You didn't tell anybody where you were going this morning," he said.

Uh-oh.

Summertime rules in the Fairmont house: One, stay out of trouble. Two, be back before the streetlights come on. And three, always let someone know where you are going to be. Three rules.

Mom and Dad were not going to be happy. And even though I think this logically shows my need for a new cell phone, I can guess that this *probably* won't be the time to ask.

Troy began to sweep just inside the bodega's front door. "So? Where have y'all been?"

"Nowhere," I said.

Troy looked up, raised an eyebrow, flashed a sly grin, and then went back to sweeping. "Sure doesn't look like nowhere. Looks like you've been somewhere. Somewhere wet, too. Did you fall into the pool again?"

"No," I said with a huff. "And that happened *one* time!" Kareem and Juan Carlos stared at me. I felt my face grow red with embarrassment.

"Okay, don't yell at *me*. I'm just asking what Mom's gonna ask. She was looking for you about an hour ago, just so you know. Something about a project for a neighbor?"

Oh poop.

I slapped my forehead. Mrs. McGee! And I'd left Handy-Bot 2.0 at the factory next to Cheese's ship. I was in big trouble.

Troy patted me on the shoulder. "Don't worry, bro. I'm sure Mom will be more focused on why you look like you took a bath with your clothes on, than on some project you've obviously forgotten about."

"Thanks, Troy," I said sarcastically.

He laughed, and I was just about to tackle him when someone shouted from across the street.

"Hey! What are you doing?" A cop marched across the street toward us, ignoring the cars that screeched to a halt as he walked in front of them. He stomped up to us and put his hands on his hips. The cop looked young, maybe a few years older than Troy, and he wore a pair of blinding sunglasses.

"Well? You all have a problem?"

"No, officer, there's no problem." Troy spoke in his voice that he saved for adults. No slang. Full sentences. It was pretty impressive. He kept both hands at his sides. I nudged Kareem and Juan Carlos to do the same.

The cop stared at each of us. It was tough to see what he was looking for from behind his sunglasses—which he honestly didn't need this late in the day—but whatever it was, he scowled when he couldn't find it.

"Well, break it up. No loitering in front of the store. Actual customers need to shop."

I looked up and down the sidewalk. We were the only ones outside at the moment. The cop noticed and took a step forward.

"I work here," Troy said calmly. "And I'm calling a ride for my brother and his friends. As you can see, they've had an accident, and I don't want them getting sick."

The cop lifted his sunglasses and narrowed his eyes. "You work here?"

"Yes, officer, I do."

Juan Carlos shifted and his shoes squelched again. Kareem snickered. I elbowed him to stop. The cop turned his gaze on us, and I could tell he was deciding if we were worth it or not. Another squelch came from behind me. The cop must've decided he was wasting his time, because he lowered his sunglasses and pointed at the middle of Troy's chest.

"Get these boys home," he said in an important voice.

Troy nodded. "I'll go call, once we're free to go."

The cop made a shooing motion, then walked across the street to confront a couple of men drinking from a brown paper bag. Troy turned his back to the cop. Instantly, the pleasant smile disappeared from his face.

The thing about neighborhoods like mine was that news traveled fast, and bad news traveled even faster. It was like the bat signal for parents went up as soon as Troy hung up the bodega phone. Kareem's dad came puttering around the corner in an old minivan. He leaned over and frowned out the window. I could feel Kareem shifting uncomfortably behind me.

Before his dad could say anything, I stepped forward and waved through the window.

"Hi, Mr. Hassan," I said.

When he turned around and saw me, his frown softened a bit.

"Hello, Ethan," he said. Mr. Hassan spoke in a quiet voice, but it was one of those parent voices that made sure you heard everything they said, 'cause they weren't going to repeat themselves. He was dark brown like my dad, but where my dad was bald, Mr. Hassan had a small Afro and a larger mustache that wriggled like a caterpillar when he spoke. "How have you been?"

"Good. Sorry for the mess," I said. Might as well get it over with. "It's my fault—I told them my invention was foolproof and . . . well, it wasn't."

The corner of Mr. Hassan's mouth twitched. "Now, why does that sound familiar?"

I scratched my head. "That time we fixed your bathroom sink? Or wait, that one time when we built that automatic lemonade maker?"

A smile spread beneath his mustache. "I was thinking of that water balloon filler you two built a few summers back."

Kareem groaned. "We had to mop the entire basement."

His dad raised an eyebrow. "And you're going to have to wipe down my van once we get home. You're dripping wet.

Come on, get in, we're late for evening prayers. It was nice seeing you again, Ethan," he said to me.

I waved. "'Bye, Mr. Hassan. Later, Kareem."

The minivan had just taken off in a cloud of smelly smoke when a loud call echoed down the street. Juan Carlos winced and looked down the block. His grandmother stood in a pair of pink slippers and a long dress with a blanket wrapped around her shoulders.

"Juanito! You're late! You were supposed to get your sisters thirty minutes ago!"

I waved. "Hi, Mrs. Hernandez. Sorry we're late."

She crossed her arms. I swear I could see her frown all the way over here. But, friends helped friends so they wouldn't get in trouble. That was my rule, and I was sticking to it.

"Hello, Ethan," she called in a stern voice.

I patted Juan Carlos on his shoulder. "I tried. Just blame me if she yells at you."

He sighed. "No, it's okay. I guess I'll see you later."

He shuffled off away as his grandmother began yelling at him down the block. Before I could begin to feel sorry for him, I heard my own name.

"Ethan Edgar Fairmont! Do you know how worried sick we were?"

Mom stalked up the sidewalk toward me and she was Mad. Capital M. I looked around for help, but Troy had disappeared inside the bodega. There was no one to stand between Mom's anger and me.

Typical.

"Sorry, Mom," I said, trying to head off the storm. "I know I should've let you know where I was going. I probably worried you sick, and I'll never do that again."

She stopped in front of me and shook her hands in front of her face as she struggled to speak. Finally, she spun around and marched back toward our house. "We'll talk about this later. Right now, I have to go check on Mrs. McGee, and *you're* coming with me. Now!"

"But, Ma. . . ."

"Don't you 'but Ma' me! Let's go!"

I dropped my head and scurried after her like my pants were on fire. All I could think about was how I'd rather stand in front of another cop for the rest of the day than face Mom's anger.

21

MRS. McGEE AND ME

Mom didn't speak as we hurried down the street toward my block.

Actually, that's not quite true.

She didn't speak to *me*. But she sure spoke to somebody. She did that thing parents do when they talk out loud to themselves, but you know they're talking about you. I walked quickly and sometimes jogged behind her to keep up as she pleaded with somebody I couldn't see.

"All I ask is for my children to think of someone other than themselves," she said just loud enough for me to hear. "Is that so hard?"

One thing to remember with Mom: don't answer those questions. Believe it or not, doing that will only get you into more trouble.

"We work so hard to make sure these kids have everything, and do they appreciate it?"

(Still don't answer.)

"And after everything we *just* talked about last night, I still have to wake up today and hunt for my son, worried sick that something's happened, only to get a call that he's being questioned by the police!"

Mom went on like that for the entire walk home. She asked questions to the air and the sky while I trudged along behind her, mouth shut and hands shoved into my damp pockets. The sun had begun to dip behind the neighborhood houses, and the shadows started to creep and stretch their greedy little hands farther and farther. As we got close to my house, a breeze blew past and I shivered.

Mom noticed and sucked her teeth. "Hurry up and go change before you catch your death of cold. And you better be back out here before I count to two!"

I've never gotten dressed faster in my life.

"*Mm-hmm*" was the only response I got when I came out in jeans and a tucked-in shirt, all the buttons buttoned to the top.

We walked two houses down and stopped in front of a one-story brick house with light blue shutters on the windows. A metal fence with weeds snaking along the bottom ran around the front yard. Mom sighed at how high the grass had grown.

"Lord help me," she whispered.

She opened the gate, and we walked up the path to a sagging wooden porch, also painted light blue. Mrs. McGee had a screen door that didn't close all the way and a heavy front door with an old-fashioned doorknob. Mom reached in her purse and pulled out a key.

"Ethan, water those flowers and then come on inside," she said before unlocking the door and stepping in the house.

I looked around and spotted two faded flowerpots perched on a small bench in the far corner of the porch. They sat in the only patch of light still filtering through the trees. Just great, I thought. When I need to be helping Cheese the most, I'm here watering plants. And I'm the last person who should be taking care of plants—I couldn't even get my greenhouse experiment to work.

"Watering the plants," I muttered. "At least with these ones, it doesn't look like I can make them *worse*."

A scraggly stalk poked out of each pot—a faded purple flower with what looked like a pine cone in the middle, and a yellow flower with droopy wrinkled petals. A battered metal watering can sat below the bench. I sprinkled a healthy amount of water on both plants, then added a bit more just to be safe. Old or not, they looked important. I wiped a bit of dirt off the pots, then stood and went inside.

Mrs. McGee's house was small and cozy. It reminded me of Grandpa Joe and Grandma Ruby's house when they'd watch me and Chris as kids. The couch and chairs all had bright flower patterns on them, there was a coffee table piled high with old magazines with famous Black people on the covers, and a thick rug blanketing the floor underneath it all. It smelled like something was always baking. I took a deep sniff and got hungry, which made me think of Cheese and I was worried all over again. The police and the Others seemed to be getting closer. We had *maybe* another day or so to get Cheese's ship fixed and on its way. The Pinball had a great hiding spot for now, but if the Others decided to search the factory again, and if they had special alien-sniffing dogs or something, then the jig would be up. But for the life of me, I still couldn't figure out how to grow light-flowers.

What was I missing?

Mrs. McGee's walls had pictures everywhere. There were pictures of a woman dancing, leaping in midair, twirling, and even one in which she stood up all the way on her toes.

Then there were pictures of Mr. McGee in an army uniform, and a picture of the two of them at their wedding. Mrs. McGee looked so happy! The two of them were dancing in each other's arms. Mrs. McGee had her head thrown back, laughing.

"Ethan Fairmont! Is that you?" a musical voice called as Mrs. McGee walked in.

No wonder Mom wanted me to come help all the time.

Mrs. McGee smiled the same brilliant smile from all her pictures on the wall as she hobbled in. She wore a colorful fuzzy knit sweater over a long dress, and she leaned on a wheeled walker that squeaked as it rolled along. Each step was slow and deliberate, as if it pained her to walk, but she held her head high and her eyes beamed as she looked at me. I felt my stomach drop, knowing I had blown off Mrs. McGee so many times before. She really did need my help.

"Boy, get over here! Looking just like your daddy. Vanessa, you didn't tell me your baby had gotten so big!"

It always felt weird hearing Mom's first name spoken out loud. Her name was Mom. Mom Fairmont.

Mom poked her head in from the kitchen. "He's getting too big. He thinks he can do what he wants."

Mrs. McGee wrinkled her nose. "Oh stop it. The boy's gotta grow into his own space, that's all. Ethan, how've you been, baby?"

"Fine," I said. Mom narrowed her eyes. "I mean, Fine, ma'am."

"And how's school going?"

"It's going good. Ma'am."

"What's your favorite subject?"

"*Uhhh* . . . science."

"That's wonderful, dear."

"Mrs. McGee, I watered the flowers on your porch, but they look like they're dying."

"Oh no, sweetie," she said. "Those are perennials. Some water and sunlight, they'll come back, just you wait. That yellow one is a Stella de Oro. Larry, my husband, loved the color yellow, so that one's for him. The other one's a coneflower. That one's for my boy, Larry Jr. He loved the way they smelled, and that flower is the last thing he bought me before he—"

Mrs. McGee cut herself off and shook her head. She finally reached the couch and tried to sit down, but her legs wouldn't stretch out and she winced in pain. I stepped over and offered an arm.

"Such a gentleman! Thank you, baby. This old dancer's legs don't work like they once did." Mrs. McGee rubbed her knee.

Mom walked out with her medical bag and crouched next to Mrs. McGee. She wrapped a strap around Mrs. McGee's arm and started squeezing a bulb attached to a hose. Then she turned a knob, and air hissed out of the strap. She patted Mrs. McGee on the arm.

"Eighty-seven over sixty. Doing better, but still not great," she said.

Mrs. McGee smiled and kept rubbing her knee. Her eyes locked on to the photos above the mantel.

"I can still remember the routine," she said softly. "Larry was there, you know. He came to each and every one of my performances. He'd buy a ticket and march down to the front row, no matter what the ticket said, and would find him a seat. And you know, Black people, we weren't allowed to sit down there! We had a balcony just for us. And that's *if* they let us in at all. But Larry didn't care. If anybody came to ask what he was doing down there, he'd pull his wallet out and show them that picture right there."

Mrs. McGee pointed to the wrinkled photo of her and her husband that sat front and center among all the others on the mantel. "He'd say, 'I watched her dance in front of me in our living room, and I'm gonna watch her dance in front of me now.'"

She smiled as tears welled in the corners of her eyes. Mom patted her arm again, then stood and began to pack up her stuff. Sirens sounded just outside the window. Mrs. McGee looked at her legs again.

"These old legs used to carry me across the stage, and now I can't even make it to the TV to change the channel," she said.

"You don't have a remote?" I asked.

"That thing hasn't worked in ages. I changed the batteries and everything, but nothing helps."

I stood up. "Can I take a look?"

Mrs. McGee raised an eyebrow. "You think you can fix it?"

"Yes, ma'am. I know I can," I said.

I mean, was I a super-genius-inventor or not?

Mom continued to pack up and chatted with Mrs. McGee as I took the remote control apart. Dust had gotten inside and covered everything, and the buttons were so sticky they didn't work right. I blew as much dust out as I could, then used the corner of my shirt to wipe the buttons off. I snapped the case back together, checked that the batteries were inserted right, then pointed it at the television.

"Good as new," I said as the evening news came on.

"Oh, that's wonderful, baby! Vanessa, you see that? Your baby fixed it like it was nothing."

"*Mm-hmm*," Mom said.

"What was wrong?" Mrs. McGee asked.

"Just a bunch of dust," I said, and she shook her head.

"Dust, dust, dust! It's always the dust, I swear. But I can't use the vacuum anymore. It's too much walking, and these old legs won't let me, but it just makes me so mad! I am not a lazy person, Ethan, I'm just not." She banged the arm of the couch with the palm of her hand and I could see her shoulders shaking with frustration. More tears were in her eyes. "Everything is just so much these days."

Mom came in, saw her distress, and immediately dropped to her knees to give Mrs. McGee a hug. The sirens grew louder. Mom had to raise her voice to be heard.

"Hush, now, you know we're here to help."

"But you can't be here all the time, Vanessa, and I don't expect you to be. You have your life to live."

"And you're a part of it, ma'am, and I won't hear any different."

Mrs. McGee snorted. "Oh, you won't hear any different, *hmm*? Where's the respect for your elders, young lady?"

"Yeah," I said, then covered my mouth as Mom shot a glare at me.

"You better go get washed up, boy," she snapped. I nearly ran to the sink.

Thoughts raced through my head as I washed my hands.

I thought about how much trouble Mrs. McGee had moving around. Handy-Bot 2.0 could do so much for her—cleaning, straightening, even just helping her walk. That old walker looked ready to fall apart.

I thought about Cheese, and Kareem, and Mrs. McGee, and how everything always seemed to come back to family.

I thought about neighborhoods, and friends, and helping each other out.

But mostly I thought about why Mom kept wanting me to come over and check on Mrs. McGee. I dried my hands and nodded to myself. As soon as I could, I'd get Handy-Bot 2.0 fixed and set it up for her. But that wasn't all. That couldn't be all. I'd come over and help, too, whether it was dusting the hard-to-reach places or just sitting and listening to more stories.

In fact—

A scream startled me.

It was Mom.

I ran into the living room, where Mrs. McGee and Mom were looking out the window.

"Mom?" I said. "What's wrong?"

She didn't answer, she just stood there and stared past the television.

"Mom?"

I moved around to see what they were looking at, then my jaw dropped open.

Police were pulling my dad out of our house. He dragged his feet and shouted over his shoulder at the cops, who held him tight. They wrestled him to the ground and handcuffed him.

I watched with horror as the man and woman in the gray suits stepped onto our porch.

The Others. They were here.

The woman held out a black metal box. My heart thudded out of my chest as I watched the suited man hold something and drop it inside the box.

The light-flower.

They'd found it.

22

THE WORST—NO, THE MOST TERRIBLE—ACTUALLY, THE ABSOLUTE MOST HORRENDOUS THING THAT COULD'VE EVER HAPPENED

The cops arrested Dad, and it was all my fault.

The cops arrested Dad, and it was all my fault.

The cops—

What was I going to do? What could I do?

The cops arrested Dad—

Whenever the cops swept into the neighborhood, it was like watching a tornado through a glass window. You stood there and watched, terrified, yet unable to turn away, and somewhere in the back of your mind you waited for the storm to smash through that glass and pull you inside.

Mom and I raced outside, while Mrs. McGee hobbled out to the porch. I'd never seen my mother so . . . so . . . I don't even know the word. She was angry and upset and crying and yelling all at the same time. There was a crowd of people surrounding the chaos in front of our house, but they parted quickly when they saw her marching up.

"What are you doing?" she asked a tall, muscular white cop writing something down in a notebook. "Ethan, stay there. HEY! Why do you have cuffs on my husband?!"

The cop didn't look up. "Ma'am, you need to step back."

"Sir, I will give you respect, but we need respect in return. This is my house, *you* need to step back, and then tell me what's going on!"

"Ma'am—"

Mom was done with him. She sidestepped the officer and headed over to a group of cops putting Dad into a police car. The tall cop looked up, saw she'd moved past him, and his eyes grew wide.

"Ma'am, you're not supposed to—"

"NO! That is my husband you're shoving in that car! What did he do? What's going on?"

Someone grabbed my shoulder. "Ethan, what's going on?"

It was Juan Carlos. I shook my head and turned back to the confusion. "They're arresting my dad!"

"What? Why?"

I looked around. Everybody was focused on Mom now. Three cops surrounded her and were preventing her from getting to the car. I lowered my voice so that only Juan Carlos could hear. "It's the Others, man. They found the light-flower."

"What light-flower?"

"I took a light-flower from Cheese's ship yesterday. I just wanted to investigate it, to find out more about the ship and what was wrong with it, but I didn't know they could track it."

"But why are they arresting your *dad*?"

I thought about that question. "He must've covered for me." The guilt hit me even harder.

"I didn't know this would happen," I said, waving my hand at everything in front of me.

A few neighborhood kids shoved past to get a better view. Juan Carlos and I moved to the side for more privacy. I kept an eye on Mom. I didn't know what was going to happen, but I'd never seen her get this angry before.

Juan Carlos stepped nervously from one foot to the other. "Oh-man, oh-man, oh-man. Oh, man. What are you going to do? This isn't good, Ethan."

"I know it's not good, dude, look! My dad is getting arrested." I felt like punching something and crying at the same time. It was my fault. All of it. If I hadn't brought that stupid light-flower, if I hadn't tried to make a robot instead of just going over to Mrs. McGee's myself. If. If. If. . . .

Mom shook her head as one cop tried to explain something to her. Mom tried to walk past him to talk to Dad. The cop put a hand on her shoulder. Mom whirled around like he'd slapped her.

"Don't touch me. Don't you dare touch me," she snarled.

Dad shouted something at Mom from inside the police car, but his words were muffled.

The cops were getting impatient. The Others had put the metal box with the light-flower into their own car. They were packed up and now ready to go. One of them, the man, whispered something to an officer, and he nodded, then shouted for everyone to move out.

"Ma'am, you can file a—"

"Don't talk to me like I don't know what's going on, I know what's going on," Mom shouted. "You take him out of that car and—"

Another cop stepped forward to usher her away, and someone shouted from the crowd:

"Hey, what are you doing to my mom?!"

Oh, no.

Chris stepped out of the crowd and headed forward. Of all us brothers, he had the worst temper, and no way was this going to end well. I started to go too, but Juan Carlos grabbed my arm.

"Dude, what are you doing?"

I shrugged him off.

"If I don't do something, they're going to arrest my whole family!" I shouted as I ran to get Chris.

That was a mistake.

"Hey!"

"Stop him!"

"Freeze!"

The magic word. The imaginary line you weren't supposed to cross, just like when a bully drew it in the dirt behind your school. Or the game you played with your friends in the neighborhood where, if you got touched, you pretended that your limbs were locked stiff.

Except this wasn't a game.

I reached Chris a few seconds before two cops did. He grunted as I nearly tackled him and dragged him away.

"Let me go!" he shouted.

"Dude, you're only going to make it worse," I said.

Somebody yelled out from the crowd, "Calm down, son." Other people nodded in agreement. I patted my brother's back but still didn't let go.

"C'mon, Chris, please."

I watched over his shoulder as the two cops approached, their hands hovering near their hips. One had a small can in the other hand.

"You two!" one of the cops snapped. "Against the fence, now!"

Chris stiffened. A tingle of dread slithered up my spine.

"Now!"

Time seemed to move slower and slower.

The Others had gone.

I knew I needed to slip off to the factory and check on Cheese, but the cops' hands were twitching. I felt the tension drain out of Chris's body. Together, we slowly moved toward the fence that ran around our house.

Somebody finally told Mom that her youngest boys were in danger of being arrested too, and she rushed over.

"Stop it, you two," she said, wiping tears from her face. "Just get back inside. Go!"

"Hold it," one of the cops said, his eyes zipping from Chris to me to Mom and back. "Now just hold it! I said move against the fence."

"Aw, man, leave the boys alone," a voice from the crowd said. People started shouting out from the crowd, and now more cops started to take notice.

"You already dragged their father out in front of them, now you wanna arrest them too?"

"Yeah!"

"Y'all should be ashamed!"

The cops, once they realized the situation had calmed, seemed hesitant. Mom grabbed Chris and me and pulled us toward the side of our house. Juan Carlos slipped through the crowd and joined us as we made our way to the front porch.

The cops dispersed the rest of the crowd while the car with Dad in it pulled off. Mom's hands tightened around me and Chris as we watched it round the corner and disappear from sight.

The story of my father's arrest quickly made its way around town. The whole neighborhood showed up to support my mom;

even Kareem and his dad came by when they heard the news. Me, Kareem, and Juan Carlos huddled on our couch in the living room. The adults were in the kitchen, comforting Mom as she cried on the phone with Grandma Ruby. I could hear Grandpa Joe in the background, his deep voice threatening to drive across town to the police station.

Juan Carlos's grandmother, Kareem's dad, Jorge, and my older brothers all stood around looking sad. Kareem's dad was going through his contacts to find a lawyer's phone number; but other than that, the whole house just felt gloomy.

"Dude, you've got to do something," Juan Carlos whispered.

I didn't answer. I held one of Dad's many aprons in my hand, twisting it and wrapping it around my arm, then unwinding it and doing the same to my other hand.

"He's right, Ethan," Kareem said from the other side. He leaned in. "People are saying your dad is tied to the fugitive they've been looking for."

"Don't," I said softly.

Kareem looked at me, his mouth open, then closed it and leaned back on the couch. I went back to twisting and untwisting the apron.

"C'mon, Ethan, you can figure this out," Kareem said, pounding my back. "You do it all the time."

"This isn't like all the other times," I snapped. "They took my dad, and it's my fault, and I can't even think right now, everything's just so wrong. It's all wrong! It wasn't supposed to go like this."

I dropped my face into my hands and squeezed.

C'mon, genius. I'm so smart, right? Just figure it out. Future mayor, right? Of Ferrous City? More like future loser of everything.

"Hey, Ethan. Stop it, man, you're freaking me out."

I looked up. Kareem held my wrist away from my face. I felt his nails digging into my skin.

"It'll be okay," he said. "But maybe we should tell the adults."

Juan Carlos winced, then nodded. "Yeah, maybe *they'll* know how to grow light-flowers."

"Wait," I said. "What did you say?"

Juan Carlos glanced at Kareem. "I was joking."

"Yeah, but what was it?"

"Maybe they'll know how to grow light-flowers."

I snapped my fingers and pointed at him. Something Mrs. McGee had said to me back at her house stuck out. *Some water and sunlight, they'll come back.* Could that be the same for the light-flowers on Cheese's ship? It was a long shot, and it'd be a lot of work; but maybe, just maybe it could work.

I looked up. "We need to go back to the factory," I said.

"What!" Kareem and Juan Carlos yelled at the same time.

Juan Carlos's grandmother and Kareem's dad looked over at us to lower our voices.

"Dude, that's what started this whole thing!" Juan Carlos whispered angrily.

"Yeah, the last thing you need to do is to go back," Kareem added.

I shook my head. "I know, but think about it. Everybody is looking for Cheese—and right now Cheese is there alone. The Others seem to have the cops working for them, and because they found that light-flower they know they're in the right spot. They're getting close."

"So?" Kareem asked. "All the more reason to stay away, right?"

"Wrong. What do you think they're going to do when they find Cheese? You think they're going to let Dad go?"

Juan Carlos and Kareem looked at each other.

"No, they're going to hush everything up. You know that. It's what they always do." I squeezed Dad's apron. He had a drawer stuffed with them, all of them with silly pictures and sayings on them. He'd started collecting them after he'd . . .

My eyes grew wide.

After he'd been let go from the factory.

The factory *was* the key.

"Guys," I said hurriedly. "I know what *to* do. But we *have* to go back to the factory, and it has to be tonight."

"Tonight?"

"After everything that just happened?"

"How—"

I stopped them both. "Do you have your candy pouch?" I asked Kareem.

"Yeah, but—"

"Good. Juan Carlos, grab that water bottle off the counter. Now leave it to me. Sometimes, like you said, you need to tell the adults."

"Mom?" I said, louder.

The talking stopped in the kitchen. Mom sniffed and wiped her eyes and smiled at me.

"Yes, baby?"

I cleared my throat. "Can I go outside with Kareem and Juan Carlos?"

Silence filled the room.

"Baby, it's very late at night. It's almost past midnight."

"Not far, just around the block. I need some air."

Mom stared at me, then looked at the other parents and neighbors. Juan Carlos's grandmother wore a frown, but I was starting to think that was just her normal expression when dealing with kids. Kareem's dad shrugged, but his eyes flicked over to his son and back again.

Mom took a deep breath. "Y'all be back here in thirty minutes."

Thirty minutes?

That wasn't enough time!

I started to ask for more, but Mom got a look in her eyes.

The Look.

I swallowed my protests and nodded.

Mom turned and answered the phone, and I turned and nodded at Kareem and Juan Carlos.

We had work to do.

23

OPERATION FIX-EVERYTHING!

We ran down the block as midnight fell on Ferrous City. It was like someone had thrown a giant blanket over our neighborhood. The streetlights barely lit our way, humming and glowing high up above like giant fireflies.

I shivered.

Juan Carlos noticed. "It's weird, right?" he asked.

"What?" Kareem asked, huffing along behind us. "What are y'all talking about?"

"The night. It feels different."

We slowed to let Kareem catch up. His chest heaved as he bent over and puffed out giant gasps. Juan Carlos stopped to wait. I sighed and stopped too. The fence separating the back of our neighborhood from the field and the abandoned factory beyond was just ahead.

Kareem wheezed, then lurched upright. "What do you mean it feels different?" he asked.

Juan Carlos waved his hands around us but didn't try to explain. I shivered again, then rubbed my arms and stared behind us. *Was that a flicker of movement?*

"Ethan?"

"*Hmm?*" I said. Both Kareem and Juan Carlos were looking at me. "Oh. Well, it's hard to describe. But, do you know how when someone's chasing you and they're getting closer, you can almost feel them about to catch you? Or, sometimes you can feel somebody watching you? That's what this night reminds me of. This whole city is blindfolded and something's looking at us, getting ready to pounce."

Kareem swallowed. "Something? You mean someone, right?"

I shrugged. "Both, I don't know."

Juan Carlos nodded, and Kareem started peeking into the shadows, just in case somebody was there. I began to tell them both to get ready to hop the fence when a flash of light twinkled in the darkness down the block.

"Did y'all see that?" I whispered.

"See what?" Kareem crouched down in the middle of the sidewalk while Juan Carlos stared at him.

"What are you doing?" Juan Carlos asked, confused.

"Hiding."

"But you're in the middle of the sidewalk. Everybody can still see you."

Kareem looked around, saw an empty flowerpot lying on its side in the grass, grabbed it and held it in front of his face.

"Hush, you two," I whispered. I stared into the darkness, trying to see if anyone was following us, like the Others, or the cops. No way was I going to lead them to Cheese. I strained my eyes, but I couldn't see anything.

"Okay, look, we need to—"

I stopped and stared at Kareem and the flowerpot.

"Kareem."

"What?"

"Get up."

He peeked out, saw both of us looking at him, and stood with a sheepish expression.

"Sorry," he said. He stood and tossed the plastic flowerpot high in the air, back the way we had come.

"Just in case anyone checks for fingerprints," he said. "I don't want them tracking us."

I rolled my eyes. "Look, we have to move, and fast: time is running out."

The flowerpot landed somewhere in the dark. Somebody yelped.

I looked at Juan Carlos, who shook his head and looked at Kareem, who shook his head and looked at me. My heart pounded at one kajillion beats per second.

A tall shadow separated from the rest of the darkness and walked forward a few steps.

We backed up.

It came closer.

We backed up farther.

It stepped into the light, and a familiar face appeared.

RJ rubbed his head with one hand, the flowerpot in the other. "What the heck? Why'd you throw that, KC?!"

Something inside of me snapped. I stopped backing up and pointed at RJ. "What are you doing here?"

RJ dropped the flowerpot and put both hands in his pockets. "I just wanted to talk."

"Talk? Are you serious?"

"Yeah, about your dad."

I balled my fists up and he quickly took a few steps back. "Don't you ever say anything about my dad again."

"Wait, just listen."

"Give him a chance, Ethan," Kareem said.

That set me off. I didn't have time for this. "Why? So he can make fun of me? 'Cause he doesn't have anything better to do *in the middle of the night*? Well, forget it, I don't wanna hear anything from him. Ever. But you can stay with him if you want—not like you didn't choose him over me before."

I turned and ran for the fence. Kareem and Juan Carlos followed after a second.

"Wait, no, it's not like that!" RJ shouted.

"Just go away!" I ducked through the fence and sprinted for the factory.

I didn't care if Kareem and Juan Carlos kept up, I just ran and ran and ran, leaping over stones and broken glass, unable to see farther than a few feet. But it didn't matter, I just ran.

The broken door that hid the secret entrance had been shoved aside. I didn't stop to think about it. I hurled myself inside. The main floor of the factory was dark, empty, and quiet. It was perfect for sprawling out on the dusty cold ground and gritting your teeth against the world. That's exactly what I did. I wiped annoying tears from out of my annoying leaky eyes and off my stupid wet cheeks and gritted my teeth.

Crying wasn't going to solve anything. The last time I checked, problems didn't care if you cried, they just waited for you to finish. And if there was one thing starting to pile up in my life, it was problems.

Dad.

Mrs. McGee.

Handy-Bot 2.0.

RJ.

Cheese.

The thought of the little floating alien dragged me to my feet. We had to get the Pinball fixed before the Others found us.

And before Mom's deadline.

I walked across the dusty factory floor and headed to the small storeroom hidden behind the machinery. The hole in the roof let moonlight spill inside.

"Hey, Cheese," I called out as I walked up to the break in the brick wall. "I think we figured out how to—"

I stopped. The Pinball looked even worse than before—the deep silver color was almost white. The entranceway opened up slowly. A tiny silver head poked out.

"Cheese!"

I ran up to the ship. Cheese looked exhausted. The black spots were back, dotting Cheese's body. Our alien floated barely an inch above the ship's entrance, wobbling and bumping into the doorway. I dropped to my knees and reached out to steady the little alien, but it felt like touching ice. Kareem and Juan ran in behind him. I have to admit, I was glad Kareem chose me.

"Guys, something is wrong with Cheese and the Pinball," I yelled.

Kareem and Juan Carlos inched their way to the ship. Cheese gave a limp fist pump to them, but otherwise leaned on me for support.

"I'm going to put Cheese down on the floor," I said.

Cheese was barely bigger than Nugget, so I cradled the alien and lowered it to the floor, then propped it in the corner. It was strange to see Cheese like this, no bobbing or twirling or anything. Kareem took off his hoodie and used it to cover Cheese like a blanket. The limp little arm reached down to the ground and scooped something up—one of the hot sauce packets I'd brought from Jorge's Bodega. Cheese brought it to his mouth and seemed to suck on it like a baby bottle.

"We have to get this ship going, both Cheese and the ship are getting weaker by the minute. Pretty soon . . ."

I shuddered at the thought.

"Never mind, we just do whatever it takes. Even if it means staying out all night."

Juan and Kareem looked at each other, terrified.

"We may not get another chance," I warned.

"But how do we fix it? We don't know a thing about this, Ethan," Kareem said. "This isn't like a radio or a vacuum or something. We don't know how this works. You can't go download the manual for a space flower-ship-thing from the Internet!"

At this, I managed to smile.

"I think I know how to grow the light-flowers."

Juan Carlos and Kareem stared at me while Cheese waved his silver arm and gave me another weak fist pump.

"How?" Kareem asked.

I walked to the wall of the ship. "Juan Carlos, come in here and empty that water bottle I asked you to bring."

He looked at me suspiciously. "Why?"

"Just trust me."

Juan Carlos still looked uncertain, but he hopped in the ship and poured his water into the gutter where the golden dust was. Nothing happened.

I looked up at the hole in the factory ceiling. *Of course.*

"Duh, there's no sun," I said to myself.

"What are you *talking* about, Ethan?"

"How do you grow flowers? Soil, water, and sunlight. I'm pretty sure the golden pollen acts as a soil and will reproduce flowers. But we need water and sunlight."

"We can't just conjure sunlight. The sun doesn't rise for another six hours.

Then it dawned on me. "Maybe we don't need the sun."

I ran to my work bench. I hadn't checked on all my old experiments since we found Cheese. I prayed the Others hadn't confiscated anything when they were searching for the alien. But nope, aside from being half covered by one of the old tarps, everything was there. I grabbed what I needed and held it up triumphantly.

"The grow-lights!" Kareem cried. "Nice!"

I raced back to the ship and connected the lamp to one of the power packs. You can never be too prepared, and this is proof.

I sat the grow-lamp down over the damp pollen as it heated up. We all took a step back and the light hit the water. The golden dust started to gyrate.

"*Whoa!* What is it doing?" Juan asked.

"Let's watch."

But I already knew what was going to happen. Cheese, as weak as he was, made a faint chirping sound under the sweatshirt.

A small metal spout popped up from the floor of the ship.

"*Whoa*, what's that?"

"It's the beginnings of a light-flower! I was right!"

It was a triumphant moment. We'd figured out how to grow the thing needed to fix Cheese's ship!

"Don't you see?" I started: "The light-flowers power the ship and the ship can grow light-flowers. It's self-sufficient. But if the ship is off, it needs sun and water, just like our flowers. Remember when I first gave Cheese water and he threw it at the ship? He was trying to tell us what it needed right then!!!"

Juan Carlos poured more water over the pollen under the grow-lamp. More small light-flowers sprouted.

"We're going to need LOTS of water," Juan Carlos exclaimed.

"And lots of grow-lamps," I added.

"Well, maybe by the time we get enough water for this whole ship, the sun will be coming up." Kareem said.

"You think it'll take that long?" asked Juan.

"There's no telling how many flowers it'll take to get this thing going," Kareem said. "We could be here for days."

Kareem was right. With just the three of us, this could be a very long process.

"What the . . . ?" a voice said from the door to the storeroom.

We all whirled around. My heart dropped into my stomach.

RJ stepped carefully into the room, like at any second something was going to leap out at him, and Di peeked from around the corner behind him.

"What is *that*?"

24

TEAMWORK, I GUESS?

I took a few steps toward RJ. I wasn't really sure of what to do next, but I knew that I couldn't let him do anything to harm Cheese or my friends. To my surprise, he backed up and raised both his hands. He looked . . . well, he looked scared.

That was a first.

"Easy, man, I'm not here to fight," he said. "Right, Di?"

Di peeked around the corner again, then stepped inside. She was wearing a green and black tracksuit, just like RJ. They almost glowed in the dark.

"Why are you here, then?"

RJ's eyes flicked from me to Cheese to the spaceship behind us. He started to say something, then paused and cleared his throat. I almost smiled. It was the first time I'd seen RJ humbled. RJ, the great RJ, looked nervous and unsure of himself. Who knew?

"This is crazy," he muttered.

Di edged around RJ and, eyeing Cheese nervously, scooted around Kareem.

"What is going on?" she whispered. "What is that?"

She pointed at the Pinball.

"And what is *that*?!" she said, pointing at Cheese.

Kareem looked at me, and I looked at Juan Carlos, but he was looking at me too.

Oh yeah. Apparently *I* was the leader.

Suddenly I was just tired of the whole thing. The broken spaceship of a tiny alien that had floated into my life a few days ago needed my help. And if I didn't help—if I *couldn't*—bad things were going to happen. To me, to my family, maybe even to all of Ferrous City. I turned away, back to the matter at hand.

"We're busy right now," I said over my shoulder. "And y'all are in the way. Why don't you just go pick on someone who cares what you think?"

"We didn't come to mess with you," RJ said.

"Then why did you come? It's the middle of the night. What are you even doing out here? You came all the way out here to harass me?" I was shouting now.

He looked away and mumbled something.

"What?" I called back.

RJ turned to me. "I said I didn't come to mess with you at all. I . . . know how you're feeling about your dad. I saw the lights on the block today and I . . . I couldn't sleep. Then I looked out my window and saw you and Kareem and the other guy passing by. So I came to tell you . . ." His voice faded out, and he cleared his throat. "I came to tell you that I'm sorry."

"Sorry? Sorry for what?"

"For everything."

I couldn't believe it. RJ apologizing? Suddenly an alien and its glowing Pinball seemed normal.

RJ stopped me in my tracks with his next words. "My dad got arrested too."

The sentence hung between us like a giant neon sign.

"RJ and Di's parents got a divorce over it," Kareem said. "When I moved, RJ was the first person I could talk to about my parents. He told me about his dad going away, his family splitting up, and about how it felt like something had been, you know, ripped away."

I felt the same thing when Dad was shoved into the police car. That achy pain that wouldn't go away, it just hovered right there in the back of my mind, ready to jump in front of me.

I turned back to RJ and scratched my head. It's not every day that you and your bully find common ground over arrested dads. Then again, it's not every day that a hot sauce-loving alien recruits you to help it fix its Pinball.

Some days are just weird.

"I'm sorry too," said Di. "My brother can be a jerk. I think it's like a coping mechanism or something, but—"

"Hey!" RJ said. But she kept going.

"—but I should've said something and not just let it happen. So, my bad."

We all stared at one another, and something about the look on Di's face made me raise my eyebrow.

"What?" I said.

She sighed.

"Look," she said. "When RJ said he saw you outside and was going to talk to you, obviously I said I was coming, too, so he didn't do anything stupid. But now that we're here . . ."

She looked pointedly over my shoulder.

I sidestepped to block her view of Cheese, scowling.

She sighed again, more dramatically this time.

"Look, clearly something weird is going on here. What *is* that? Is that a robot you built or something? We saw the cops searching this place yesterday morning when I was running laps. And now here you are. What's the deal?"

One look at RJ told me that he was thinking along the same lines as his sister.

"Wait, did you even come to apologize?" I yelled. "Or are you just here to be nosy?!"

RJ shook his head. "Look, it's more complicated than that. And I *am* sorry. Seeing what happened to your dad has me in my feelings. But I'd be lying if I said I wasn't wondering what you're up to. My dad got arrested because of cops finding excuses to bother Black folks. Now the cops are combing through our neighborhood; meanwhile, you and your friends are doing something shady in the same spot the cops were searching? And you're sneaking down the side-walk at midnight? I don't want any more beef with you, but I also need to know what's going on. This stuff with the cops is . . . scary."

I tilted my head back, looking at the ceiling to keep tears from falling. This is exactly why I needed to get Cheese out of here ASAP. For his sake and ours.

"It's really complicated," I said.

Di raised her eyebrow. RJ frowned. He didn't look mean. He looked worried.

"It's not a robot," I said, sighing. "It's an alien."

They stared blankly at me, RJ squinting like he thought I was playing a joke. I stepped to the side and pointed at the Pinball.

"Are you serious?" RJ looked at Cheese, who decided in that moment to issue a small fist pump to the newcomers.

"This is Cheese," I said. "This little alien is running from a bully of its own, and it's trying to get back to its family. But it can't do that without our help. So that's what we're doing. Helping."

"Who's 'we'?" RJ asked. "Y'all?"

"Yes," I said, then paused. "And if you really care about our neighborhood, you'll help too."

Di narrowed her eyes. "What kind of help?" she asked.

I grinned. Kareem groaned. After a second, Juan Carlos groaned too. He figured out what Kareem already knew.

"We need water for the ship," I explained. "You know the river that runs alongside Gadget Beach?"

"I can find it." RJ extended his hand, a sign of good faith.

My pride wanted to leave him hanging, but there was something bigger at stake. We shook on it, and suddenly I had a good feeling.

We worked like nothing else mattered. When there were only three of us, fixing Cheese's ship felt like it would never happen, like we were naive just to think we could. But now, with RJ and Di, it felt like we could actually do this, like we were a team.

First, I made a plan to amplify the power of the grow-lights I had from my failed miniature greenhouse project. My power packs would be useful, but we needed other stuff—extension cords, and any power conduits we could find. Luckily, the Factory was the perfect place for scavenging, mostly because of all the junk I'd already brought in here. We raided my work-bench, and together we assembled what I privately called Ultra Grow-Lights: the grow-lamps amplified with my power packs, aimed at Cheese's ship like its own personal sun.

Second, we made a plan to pull water from the river. We didn't need to go all the way to Gadget Beach to get to the river, but we did need a gadget to speed up the process of getting the water from the river up the dirt road and into the factory. In the end, remembering what I'd read about Occam's Razor made it easy: sometimes for the sake of efficiency, the simplest plan is the best one. So we tipped over a plastic barrel that I'd stowed under my workbench (which I'd intended to use for the greenhouse project) and Kareem, RJ, and Di rolled it down to the river. Rolling it back full of water was harder, but it was faster than going back and forth a billion times. Then it was just a matter of pouring it out into buckets, which we found in the supply closet. Simple.

"So what's the water *for?*" Di asked, rubbing her aching shoulders. RJ was still catching his breath.

"We water the ship," I said.

I poured several buckets of water into the ship. Finally the entire gutter, the one I'd slipped into the first time, was covered in water. The golden pollen hardened into a gel that sort of looked like rubber. Small sprouts of metal light-flowers began to pop up under the Ultra Grow-Light, but even with the amplification, the glow only covered a very small section of the ship.

"They aren't growing fast enough, Ethan," Juan said.

I rolled my eyes. "Yes, I see." Ultra or not, the lamps just weren't strong enough.

I looked at the hole in the ceiling and could see the morning sky starting to peek through the darkness. I looked at the east wall of the factory and the boarded-up windows. I'm not sure how long we had been working, but it was almost morning.

I had a sick feeling thinking about my mom, how worried she must be. But I would explain everything as soon as I could.

"One more piece to this puzzle," I said.

I hadn't really noticed before, but the ceiling directly around where the Pinball had crashed through was unstable. Wood and metal dangled as if the entire section of the roof could cave in at any moment.

"I've got an idea. Follow me."

We got off the ship, and I ran over to the metal scraps we had left over from Gadget Beach and fashioned a capsule launcher, which is really just a slingshot, but I like "capsule launcher." I took aim at the roof and fired.

The screw I was using as a projectile went a few feet in the air, then dropped. Embarrassing.

"Here, let me try," RJ said. He walked over and grabbed the weapon from me. He picked up the screw and loaded the capsule launcher. He took aim, fired, and the screw hit the ceiling with a thud.

"*Whoa!*" we all exclaimed. It was a great shot.

RJ turned around with a proud look on his face. "I get a lot of pract—"

"Watch out!" I heard myself scream.

A piece of the ceiling came crashing down where the Pinball once had been. Glad we'd moved it to its hiding spot.

I fanned in front of my face as dust filled the air. Then I noticed something else: I could see more of the sky. As tired as I was, I felt suddenly awake. It was time to get busy.

"Okay, RJ. You finish here. Juan, Kareem, you two move any pieces that fall in the way of the ship. We don't know what its take-off pattern is like, and we don't want it to have any obstacles when it's time to bust out. But be careful. Di, come with me."

Di and I raced to the east end of the factory where the boarded-up windows were.

"You think you can break through these?"

Di smirked. "Just watch me."

She ran over and started shattering windows and kicking out the wood planks that blocked the sun. Rays of sunlight poured into the factory. A small sprout of a light-flower grew higher and stronger. Another sprout popped up beside it.

"It's working! We need more light!" I yelled.

We started moving faster. I grabbed anything I could reach and threw it at the ceiling to help RJ open up the roof. I threw things at the windows too, as Di kicked out the boards nailed down from the other side.

It was a wild sight: me, Kareem, Juan Carlos, RJ, and Di, ripping and running throughout the factory, tossing stuff around and dodging falling debris. We were yelling, screaming, laughing; and all the while, more and more sunlight flooded into the warehouse and onto the spaceship. No parents telling us to stop, no police trying to lock us up. Just kids having fun.

We all seemed to stop at the same time, huffing and puffing. It started to get hard to breathe with all the dust in the air. But by the time we were done, we'd cleared all the windows on the east side of the factory. A steady stream of sunlight beamed straight onto the Pinball.

"Come on, let's check the ship," I said.

We crowded around the Pinball and peeked inside. Hundreds and hundreds of light-flowers were blooming in the streambed around the ship. Light-flowers of every color: gold, silver, purple, you name it!

"They're growing, Ethan! You fixed it!" Juan Carlos cheered.

"Not quite. We still have to feed these to the ship. Like gas to a car. Where is the gas tank?"

I didn't need to figure that part out. When I looked up, Cheese was carrying a flower back over to his control panel. He pressed a button and the panel lifted, revealing a space just big enough for a light-flower. Cheese put the flower in, then I felt something weird. The ship seemed to wake up as it jolted forward, knocking us all backward.

"*Now* I think we fixed it," I said.

Cheese spun and spun and spun faster than I'd ever seen him spin. He bobbed so hard, I thought he'd pass out.

I'm not going to say I wanted to cry, but there was definitely something in my eye.

25

TIME TO GO

The Pinball hummed with energy as we loaded flowers into the control panel. The light-flowers just kept growing. A beautiful garden exploded inside the ship. Different colors splashed around the room, like fireworks bursting in complete silence. Emerald green, ruby red, dazzling yellows, and ocean blues— the colors filled the room.

"It's like I'm standing inside a rainbow," Juan Carlos whispered.

Di shook her head. "It's like swimming in a disco ball."

RJ stood still while his eyes raced around the room, eager to see more.

Kareem rubbed his stomach. "It's like I'm trapped in a jar of sprinkles."

I was just plain speechless.

Cheese turned around and twirled so fast that little dust clouds began to move around it. The alien chirped as it spun through the air. The only thing I could think of was the picture of Mrs. McGee leaping across the stage.

"What's it doing?" RJ asked nervously.

"Dancing," I said.

"Why?"

"Because it gets to see its family."

The golden dust swirled in little midair streams, curling around Cheese before being absorbed by the control room's equipment. Things started to glow, making the room even more magical. The giant display on the control panel flickered to life, light-flowers blinked in colorful patterns, and the floor started to rumble beneath my feet.

Cheese celebrated as the Pinball came alive. The alien zipped around us, giving fist pump after fist pump.

"*Wooo!* Go, Cheese," I shouted.

Kareem started clapping, and Juan Carlos skipped around the room. RJ and Di looked at us like we were aliens!

"What's next?" Kareem asked.

"I guess it'll be time for goodbyes." The reality stung.

Kareem nodded, slow and sad.

"I'm going to miss the little dude," Kareem said.

"Me too, man. Me too," I said. "I'll never look at a pickle the same again."

"Pickle-gurrfurr," Kareem said softly.

"Yeah. Pickle-gurrfurr."

As if the Pinball recognized *pickle-gurrfurr* as the signal to leave, several light-flowers started blinking a pattern along the wall.

Silence stretched throughout the control room. I cleared my throat and pointed at the door. "Looks like it's time for us to go," I said softly.

Cheese twirled gently.

Kareem smiled, then pulled a hot sauce packet from his pocket and dropped it in Cheese's only hand.

"For the road," he said.

Juan Carlos patted Kareem on the shoulder, then took his place. He knelt down in front of Cheese.

"For the love of—"

"Here, Cheese," Juan Carlos said, cutting me off. "For the road." He stood up and held out his right shoe, standing there wearing one big blue shoe and a holey sock.

"What is that supposed to mean?" Di whispered to Kareem.

"I'll tell y'all later," he whispered back.

Cheese looked at RJ, who swallowed and shook his head. Di sort of waved when Cheese turned her way, but she didn't say anything either.

Then the little dude pointed at me.

"Famolee," Cheese said.

"Did it just say—?" Kareem started to ask.

"Yeah, I think so," I said.

"Yes, Cheese. We are family. Now let's get you home."

I asked everyone to stand back so that I could watch as Cheese—no, as Chzwrzkrnpop—prepared to blast off. I'd miss the little dude. It had only been a few days, but already it felt like Cheese was as much a part of our group of friends as anyone else.

The Pinball shook, then began to hum louder. I stepped toward the ramp and held my hands over my ears. A terrifying rattling sound came from outside. The metal scraps still on the assembly line must've been shaking like crazy.

"Famolee," came a shout from behind me.

I turned and grunted as Cheese barreled into my stomach. It took me a second to realize what it was doing; but when I did, I bit my lip and threw my arms around it.

Aliens are stupid, and so are eyes.

"Thank you," Cheese said quietly, giving me a one-armed alien hug.

"You're welcome, buddy," I half-sobbed. "You're welcome."

I pulled away and quickly wiped away the tears. Cheese floated back to the ship and gave me a fist pump. I laughed and sniffled, then imitated it.

"Right back at you, dude," I said.

"All right, y'all," I shouted above the noise outside. "Everybody say goodbye to Ferrous City's first and last alien. I—"

I froze at the bottom of the ramp. Luckily, I'd just stepped off, 'cause a second later it disappeared back up into the Pinball. My focus wasn't on the ramp, though. It was on the two adults in sunglasses and gray suits standing at the storeroom door.

The Others.

26

THE LIGHT-THIEVES

One of them held a large lockbox like the one they'd used to contain the light-flower they'd confiscated from my house. The other stood over my friends, arms outstretched. Both of them were looking at the Pinball. One of them, the man, licked his lips. I took a step, and their eyes snapped to me. The one holding the lockbox, the woman, hissed.

"Tell the little one to come out," she said.

I looked at Kareem and Juan Carlos, RJ, and Di. I puffed my chest out and stood tall. "Or what?" I tried to sound tough.

"Tell the little one to come out now," the man repeated. He didn't add an "or else." He just took off his sunglasses and smiled.

My heart skipped a beat. I slapped my hand over my mouth just in time to muffle a scream.

"Ethan, what's wrong?" Kareem called.

I didn't answer.

"Ethan?" Juan Carlos said. "Are you o—"

The man turned his smile on them. Juan Carlos yelped and went silent. RJ squealed.

These weren't what we believed to be Others at all. They weren't even human. They were imposters!

The woman took her sunglasses off too, and she had the same all-white eyes with green specks floating in them. She smiled and bared thin, noodle-like teeth.

"Light-thieves," I whisper-yelped.

The rattling noise started to become unbearable as the entire factory shook. The man and woman—no, the *light-thieves*—hissed and stalked forward. Their skin peeled at the neck, and their feet popped out of their shoes. They hunched over and screeched as the seams of their suits tore apart. Shape-shifters, just like Kareem had said. They shed their disguises as they approached Cheese's ship. I scanned the room, desperate for anything to help us, to help Cheese, but it seemed hopeless. I hated to imagine Cheese in the Pinball, watching the creatures who had hurt his family closing in.

Then I realized that the light-thieves were still in the shade. Above them, a huge metal plank was on the verge of free-falling.

"RJ, you think you can hit that plank?"

"I know I can. Tell me when."

RJ readied the capsule blaster.

The light-thieves grew as they transformed into their true forms. They hissed and clawed as they crept toward the ship. But they weren't close enough.

"Now?" RJ cried.

"Not yet."

They got closer.

"Now?!"

"Not YET!"

The light-thieves stretched out as the wings on their back started to unfold. They were just about to step into the sunlight.

"NOW!" I yelled as RJ let the slingshot go.

Time slowed as we watched the screw shoot through the air. It hit the ceiling with a thud, and the metal plank started to slide.

The light-thieves leaped from their back feet, mouths wide and ready to chew through the Pinball and devour Cheese.

I closed my eyes.

SQUISH!

Something wet splattered on my jeans.

I opened my eyes. The metal plank had fallen, leaving two giant, dark splotches on the ground. Kareem gagged, and everyone else looked shocked and squeamish.

"Did that really just happen?" I asked, stunned.

"Unless my eyes are deceiving me," Kareem said.

"Is *anyone* going to explain what the heck that *was*?!" Di demanded.

"Remember I said Cheese had bullies?" I said slowly. "Um . . . that was them."

"Those two came all the way across the galaxy for little Cheese," Juan Carlos said mournfully.

"I'm seriously going to need therapy," RJ muttered.

Then the Pinball kicked on.

We covered our eyes as Cheese's ship shrunk for liftoff. It rose to the ceiling, and then it was off, firing through the hole in the roof and into the sky.

A sudden quiet filled the room. The rattling was gone.

Finally, Juan Carlos broke the silence. "*Eeew*, not again! I've got alien gunk on my foot, and it smells awful."

Kareem grinned. "Poop zombie returns!"

EPILOGUE

The afternoon sun peeked through the repaired windows high in the factory ceiling. I stood on a temporary stage in the middle of the floor, curtains blocking me from everyone's view. I tightened the straps on my Piggy Pack and moved my head from side to side.

"Okay, Nugget. You ready?"

Someone tapped me on the shoulder. I turned around to find Di standing there, her arms crossed, one foot tapping.

"Ready?" Di asked. She was wearing a white blouse with a navy blue skirt. Her eyes dared me to say anything but *yes*.

"*Um* . . . yes."

"Good. They're waiting." She walked with purpose toward the curtains. Just before she stepped through, she whirled around.

"What?" I gulped.

"Well?" she said. "How do I look?"

"Oh, *um*. You look . . . nice?"

Di stared at me, then slipped through the curtains. I heard her start to introduce me. I let out a sigh of relief and loosened my collar. If you thought aliens were confusing, wait until you meet a sixth-grade girl.

"—Ethan Fairmont!" Di finished, and the curtains pulled back.

The crowd was huge. It looked like all of Ferrous City had come! Mom and Dad sat in the front row along with Ant, Troy, and Chris. My brothers snickered when they saw the Piggy Pack on my head. Ms. Hernandez sat next to them, and Kareem's parents sat on the other side. Jorge sat behind them. He raised both hands in victory when he saw me. I couldn't help but grin. My smile grew even wider when I saw who was at the end of the aisle.

Mrs. McGee sat in her new wheelchair, waving at me as I walked to the edge of the stage. She dabbed at her eyes, and a rush of energy swept through me—if she could make it here, I could give a puny little speech.

I took a deep breath, then picked up the microphone.

"Ladies and gentlemen, thank you for coming to the grand opening of Ferrous City's first, but I hope not the last, Create Space. The Factory is back!" I let a round of applause fill the air, then gestured to the side of the stage where Kareem, Di, RJ, and Juan Carlos all stood. "Before we demonstrate the first project completed here, let me introduce the team. . . ."

Six weeks had passed since Cheese had left, and life was starting to go back to normal. I was finally allowed to leave my room again after giving my family such a scare by being out all night fixing Cheese's ship. We told them we had gone to the factory and had fallen asleep. (At least it was partially true.) They actually bought it, even though we still got in lots of trouble.

The most important thing to happen? The cops released Dad from jail. Once Cheese left, the Others disappeared. The cops didn't understand why those "special agents" had left without notice after the supposed importance of the "fugitive" they were looking for. With "the Others" and their case gone, the police had no cause to hold Dad, so he walked out a free man. We even got an apology from the city.

Mom is still talking about a lawsuit, but the day he came home Mom kissed Dad so hard and for so long that I took a nap and woke up and they were still standing and kissing. I mean, give me a break, am I right?

Speaking of Mom, she helped me put together the wheelchair for Mrs. McGee. I added a few enhancements, of course. Let's just say that our neighbor can go from zero to sixty down the block if she wants to. Mom rolled her eyes when she saw it, but she let it slide because Mrs. McGee rarely had to use it. Instead, I pushed her on her daily walks.

I enjoyed our visits. We talked about dancing (pretty cool), school (sort of boring), and girls (why?). But mostly we talked about my inventions. Ever since I set up Handy-Bot 3.0 for her, Mrs. McGee has been fascinated with my inventions.

Oh, what's new about Handy-Bot 3.0?

Well, to tell you the truth, I'm not really sure. I mean, I know what's different, and the robot has some cool new features, but I didn't do them.

That's right.

As soon as I was off punishment, I snuck into the factory one afternoon to pick up some spare parts from my stash, only to find a completely fixed, brand-new robot waiting for me. Next to it, on the floor, sat an empty packet of hot sauce.

Aliens are the best, even if they're weird.

So now my team worked on building more Handy-Bots for others like Mrs. McGee. I couldn't have done it without them, despite all our problems in the beginning—when we were together, weird, crazy, magical things happened.

"First up," I said to the crowd, "the one-shoe wonder himself, Juan Carlos!"

The crowd cheered as Juan Carlos walked up to the middle of the stage. He still wore his cousin's shoe on his right foot, but on his left foot he wore a fuzzy pink slipper. His grandmother didn't mess around. He waved and then quickly moved to stand behind Kareem.

"Next, she's quick on the court and even quicker to tell you about it, Di!"

Di sneered at me, then waved to the crowd and stepped back.

"Next, you know who it's gotta be, from a stick in the mud to turning a new leaf, it's RJ!"

I ducked a halfhearted punch from RJ as he shuffled forward and growled something threatening at me. But, like, I gotta get my shots in somehow, right?

"And finally, no snack is safe when this dude's on the case, it's Ka-reeeeeeeeem!"

The crowd cheered as Kareem trotted forward and we dapped up. I heard Mom cheering extra-loud, and Kareem's father and my dad smiled from ear to ear. I let the team enjoy the cheers for a few more seconds, and then I raised my arms to shush everybody.

"All right, all right, it's time for y'all to see what all the fuss is about. Everyone ready?" Kareem and Juan Carlos nodded, and as RJ and Di wheeled Handy-Bot 3.0 forward, they dumped buckets of dirt and bits of trash on the floor. The crowd started to murmur.

They were in for a treat.

My name is Ethan Edgar Fairmont. I'm a super-genius-inventor, future mayor of Ferrous City; and right now I wanted nothing more than to be here, in front of my friends and family.

"Handy-Bot, clean."

ACKNOWLEDGMENTS

First and foremost I want to thank my incredibly supportive wife. Thank you for being patient with me, encouraging me and graciously listening for hours on end as I rattle off random story ideas. I want to thank my two, new, beautiful, twin baby girls. You have ignited a fire in me I didn't know existed. I'd like to thank my mother, father, and grandparents for curating a set of experiences that made me the man I am today. Without your intentionality, maybe I'm not writing these acknowledgments today.

Thank you to Joanna Volpe, who I like to think "discovered" me. You are incredibly good at what you do, the playmaker of all playmakers. The proof is in the pudding. Thank you to Dhonielle Clayton who believed in me enough to give me the shot I've always needed. I'm forever grateful. Thank you, Dhonielle, for breaking down barriers in this industry and building a platform that has allowed so many voices to shine. Thank you to Tracey Keevan for taking a chance on a young author and recognizing the charm and heart of Ethan. Thank you to the teams at New Leaf, Cake Creative, and Union Square Kids. Thank you to Godwin Akpan, Emily

Meehan, Melissa Farris, Whitney Manger, Marcie Lawrence, Suzy Capozzi, Sam Knoerzer, Renee Yewdaev, and Hannah Reich. Without you all, ETHAN could not be possible. This has been such a great community of extremely smart people who believe in the power of storytelling.

And lastly I want to thank all the students I've ever taught, or passed in a hallway, or coached in little league. You all have inspired me in so many ways and I'm working to return the favor. You can be anything in this world you want to be, your imagination is one of your biggest assets, take advantage!

With much love, thank you all.

–Nick